Three
Witches

J.M.Clerkin

Copyright © 2024 by J.M. Clerkin
ISBN: 978-1-9161030-1-6

For more information contact: jmclerkinstories@hotmail.com

For September, chai tea, and bagels

August 25th

I shut the red gate in front of our house. My mother watched from the sitting room window with one hand holding onto the lace net. She blew a kiss. I caught it and put it into my pocket. Then I blew her my own kiss. Even though the netting obstructed my view, I knew Mam would catch that kiss and stamp it on her heart. The net ruffled just as the kiss was stamped in place.

Our house was the most nondescript house on a nondescript street full of two-ups and two-downs, many of which had extensions. Our home did not. I once asked Mam and Dad if we could get an extension. They said there was no need when it was just the three of us living there. I suspected that they liked fitting into the point of being invisible. Two years ago, I tried to do something about the house's blandness by installing window boxes on every windowsill. It worked until I went to visit my relatives in Donegal for a fortnight over the summer, and the flowers wilted during the summer heatwave. I could have replanted them, of course, but I didn't. It would have been all too much to bear if they died again. Mam thinks I'm overdramatic like that. I guess that's why I'm studying drama.

The window boxes with their dead flowers were still on the windowsills. I glanced at them before I began my journey to the bus stop. There was a thin film of sweat on my hands. I wiped them on my black shorts—the same colour as my T-shirt. Mam asked me if I, at twenty-one, was going through a teenage goth stage. I told her I was no longer a teenager and that black was a common colour for actors to wear when getting into character.

"But you're not getting into character for anything at the moment, are you?" Mam asked.

She wasn't joking, but the question still annoyed me. "What is life but one great act? And you know I'm starting my final year soon; this is my way of preparing for it."

"Whatever makes you happy," Mam said.

Mam's words rang in my head. The street was loud with traffic and people as they bustled home from work. When I was a child, the soundtrack of late summer came from the sounds of children and lawnmowers. Now, the children on the street were grown, and the gardens were mostly filled with tarmac.

I hit the button on the pedestrian crossing and counted the cars as they sped past. Waiting for the lights to change colour always frightened me. Not that I have any intention of doing so, but it would be incredibly easy just to take one small step and bang; either I'd be crippled or dead.

I squeezed my eyes shut. Summer wind blew on my slightly sunburnt cheeks. When I opened my eyes again, the lights had turned green. The bus stop came into view when I turned the corner. A few people were waiting there. One of them I knew from college. We were both Theatre Studies majors at the Celtic Technological University.

"Lacey!" He smiled when he saw me—a wide smile with uneven, white teeth. A man stood next to him with dark brown hair and dark eyes.

"Hi Gary," I said.

"Are you going to the fireworks?" He asked. He leaned into me. No matter how loud I spoke, Gary was forever creeping closer. You wouldn't think he'd need to do so with those huge ears attached to his egg-shaped head.

I nodded. "I go every year."

"Are they any good?" the dark-haired man asked. He had a good voice, not too loud or soft. Gary's was like a squeal.

"They are," I said.

"This is Ben," Gary said. "We went to school together."

"I've never seen you around before," I said. Castlebridge was by no means tiny, but you'd still recognise people unless they spent all their time hiding inside. Ben didn't have the look of a hermit though.

"I left straight after sixth year, but I just moved back last month."

Well, that explained things then. "Moved back from where?"

"Dublin. I was living right near Temple Bar. Rent went through the roof, so I had to come home. Are you studying Theatre Studies too?"

"I am," I said.

"Well, now, isn't that something? I'm looking for actors. I've already roped Gary in."

"He has," Gary said. "Though he'll probably put me in

as one of the Three Witches in his play." Gary thought he was being funny, but I didn't know what he was talking about.

"It's not my play," Ben said. "I'm just directing it."

"You're a director?" I asked.

"Trying to be anyway," Ben said. "That, combined with the rent, incited me to return. Save the two-hour commute during rehearsals."

"And what play are you going to be putting on?"

"Macbeth. Or I should say, The Scottish Play?"

The bus turned the corner at the top of the road. Gary's eyes bulged when he saw it. "Here we are, lads."

"Oh, Macbeth! We studied it in the first year of college." I remembered having a particularly bad hangover that day. I'd only gone in cause Mam was raging at me for coming home in the horrors the night before. If I had stayed in the house any longer, my ears would've bled.

"So, you must know it pretty well then?" Ben asked.

"Well enough," I said. "Although I chose not to focus on it for my exam." To tell the truth, I couldn't even tell you what I did choose. During my first year, exams weren't my priority.

"Lads, here's the bus," Gary repeated as the bus pulled

up alongside us.

"I hope you'll audition for it," Ben said.

"I might." Of course, I'd audition. He'd be mad to think I wouldn't.

"I bet you'd make a great Lady Macbeth."

The bus's doors slid open, bringing with it a gasp of warm air smelling of sweat, overly sweet perfume, and beer. I handed my fare to the driver.

"Lacey," Jess called. She waved to me with her ring-infused hand, and the bangles on her wrist jangled.

Her headful of red curls, made frizzy from the humidity of the day, framed her oval face. The heat in the bus gave her face a slightly reddish colour.

"What was that all about?" Jess asked when I sat down. Even with the multitude of aromas surrounding me, I still got a familiar whiff of patchouli and lavender from Jess. I swear she must dowse herself in the oils.

"What was what all about?"

"I saw you were talking to Ben—I didn't know you were friends with him."

"Oh, I'm not—"

"More than friends then?"

"We just met at the bus stop. He knows Gary."

"You fancy Ben," Jess said, playing with a silver ring that had the triple Goddess symbol on its front. The ring was new. She must spend a fortune on her jewellery.

Jess was forever telling me things about myself that she thought I knew. "Do your spidey senses tell you so?"

"Just be careful," Jess's large, almost bug-like eyes met my green almond-shaped ones. "He's a regular old Byron."

"So, he's a bit of a ladies' man?" I searched through the crowd and found him talking to a brunette in a tight pink jumper.

"Did you and him ever?" I asked.

"Once, many moons ago."

This didn't surprise me in the least. Jewellery wasn't the only thing Jess was passionate about. "Speaking of the moon, it's full tonight, right?"

Jess pushed one of her strands of flyway hair behind her ear. "It is. Full moon and the weirdoes are out."

The bus eased its way through the loops and bends of Moonbay East. In the distance, I could see the bright light from the Sturgeon Moon claiming the still sea's surface.

"She's so beautiful," Jess whispered.

"Who is?" I asked, looking around the bus for the

suspected beauty.

"The moon," Jess said.

"I guess it does look quite pretty tonight."

"Quite pretty? Now, that's the understatement of the year. People never appreciate just how wonderful the moon is. In ancient times, the moon's significance was known by all."

"You're talking like the moon has a soul," I said.

"Everything on this earth has a soul. That's the problem with the modern times that we live in; people have lost their relationship with the earth. Although people are awakening, it's the age of Aquarius, baby."

The bus pulled into the station. I no longer felt like a sardine stuffed in a tin can as people slipped out into the electric night. Jess and myself walked to the funfair and the surrounding seashore.

A plethora of multicoloured lights lit up the diving into dusk night sky. Chief among them and standing in originality were the silver lights belonging to the big wheel. A ride so tall that it was rumoured to be the very vessel that brought people to the heavens when death came to claim them. In the distance, close to the water's edge, stood the old creaking rollercoaster that broke down as often as it worked. Its slopes were hills rather than mountains, but this and its indecision not to work did not deter people from riding it. It only seemed to edge them on, knowing that the rollercoaster could endanger their lives. Tucked inside the confines of the main amusement park were the softer rides. That's where Jess and myself were strolling when she grabbed my hand.

I let myself be led away. A part of me wished I could always follow and not have to make the decisions that being an adult required. Jess was good at making decisions, even if most of them were questionable.

"Where are you dragging me?" I asked as we passed by the waltzer cars.

"You won't know if you don't follow me," Jess yelled.

"Why does that sound like a warning?" I screamed, but Jess either didn't hear or chose not to answer.

A grey skeleton head fuming green smoke from its nostrils announced the presence of the ghost train. Jess's rapid walking slowed; over her shoulder, she said, "Don't suppose you'd care to join me on the ghost train, would you?"

When I was a child, I had an awful experience on it; I convinced myself that the clown mannequin was following me around the ride. It turned out it was just one of the young fellas paid to frighten the customers by tapping them on their shoulders. I used to dream about the clown for years after it. "Not today."

"You're not scared, are you? I bet if Ben were here, you'd only be jumping into his lap."

"More like you would," I said. She would and all if she thought I was into him. Last year, I'd a thing for the young fella who worked in the garage near the college, and as soon as I told Jess, she went after him. I didn't talk to her for a whole month afterwards. Jess might be all with her love and light, but she can be a real madam when she wants to be.

We walked to the gate that enclosed the funfair. A train, loved by children and adults alike, travelled every ten minutes around the perimeter. The gate that fed people in and out of the park was directly on its line; to avoid a collision, the park manager had installed a novelty set of traffic lights. The lights turned green as we approached, and we walked across the train tracks.

We passed the line of people waiting to board the train and ran past them towards the sound of waves and street vendors.

Cascades of lights hung from the lampposts with their dull silver bulbs, giving enough visibility to show the large, somewhat garish mural of a dolphin. However, most of the murals were covered by street vendors selling anything from hot foods to wood name carvings.

My stomach rumbled with the smell of all the different foods. I hadn't eaten dinner yet. A lady with purple hair working in a pastry truck dipped a doughnut into a cauldron of melted chocolate. My mouth salivated.

"I smell pretzels and doughnuts," I said.

"I smell fortune and magic," Jess said. "But first, vodka."

"That's an odd mixture."

"Not really." Jess opened her green bag and took out a silver flask with a pentagram engraved on its front.

"You can't be bringing that around with you." Or more like shouldn't—she was already well on her way to developing an alcohol problem. That's if she didn't have one already.

Jess, unperturbed, unscrewed the lid and took a sip of the spirit. "What's the matter? We're not underage, and everyone drinks on the street tonight!" She took another drink and handed me the flask.

"Can we at least try to conceal what we're doing?"

"Oh, come on, Lacey!" Jess said. "It'll only take you a second."

"Fine." I took a sip from her flask. "That's disgusting." It was; I could feel it burning the back of my throat. "I don't know how you're able to drink it raw like that."

"It's easy," Jess grabbed the flask and took another long drink.

"You'll have nothing left before the night is out."

"Well, there's still plenty of time to get more drink if that's what needs to be done. Now, are you ready for your future to be revealed?" Jess's dark blue eyes looked black.

"I know what my future holds. After this year in college, I'll leave Castlebridge and do my Masters in Dublin. Then I'll travel the world on the stage."

"I know your plan, but how about we see if it's valid?"

"Oh, I know it's a valid plan when the intentions are there. I can't possibly fail now, can I?" Jess never came right out and said it, but I knew she didn't believe in me as an actor—just as well my self-belief wasn't determined by her opinion.

"There's a woman over there." Jess pointed to a caravan with a large sign outside saying Madam Lee, seventh daughter of a seventh daughter."

"I'm not sure."

Jess waved her flask in front of my face. "Do you need courage?"

Even with the taste of vodka rank in my mouth, I drank once again. The second sip wasn't as bad as the first. "My mother says you're a bad influence on me; do you know that?"

"I am a bad influence; make no mistake about that. Now, are you ready to find out if you and Ben will have two perfect children and live on a farm somewhere?"

"Ben? Byron Ben."

"The one and only. Let's see if your dreams and destiny are on the same path."

"I hardly think that Ben is anywhere in my destiny; he's hardly the settling down kind, now is he?"

"Why not get your cards read and find out?"

"Why don't you just read my cards for me then?" Jess was a self-proclaimed 'card-slinger.' Sometimes, I let her read for me. She never gave me good news, so I had this little game with myself that I'd just accept the opposite of what she said.

"I could, but wouldn't it be fun to try it with someone

you don't know?"

"I guess it would," I said.

Jess took a box of cigarettes out of her green handbag. "Care to take a journey with me into the future?" She fished out a lighter from her leather jacket and lit the tip of her cigarette before taking a long inhale.

"Okay," I said. "Let's do it."

There was little dirt on the caravan's exterior, just the regular stains and road dust that one would expect from a travelling fortune teller.

Jess knocked on the door. It opened a heartbeat later, and a woman, somewhere in her fifties with auburn hair and bright green eyes, filled the doorway.

"How are ye, girls?" Before either of us could answer, she added, "Are ye looking to get a reading?"

"We most definitely are," Jess said. She blew smoke out the side of her mouth. "How much are the readings?"

"Ah, don't worry about the price. You'll pay what you can afford, but nothing less than ten euros. How does that sound?"

"That sounds about right," Jess said. "My friend will go first; she's keen to get her reading done."

I wasn't, but I followed the smiling Madam Lee into her

caravan. It smelled like chai tea and the cinnamon incense that was burning on the countertop. There was a screened-off area at the back of the caravan with posters of several major arcana from the tarot on the flimsy door. Madam Lee asked me to sit down on a seat on either side of a fold-up table. I did, and she joined directly across.

"What would you like me to do for you today?"

"What are the options," I asked.

"Tarot cards, palm reading, or I could read your tea leaves?"

Jess and I had tried to learn palm reading before, but neither of us was good. And tea leaves, neither of us had even tried. "How much for the palm reading?"

"€10, and for €20, I'll include a Celtic Cross reading."

I took the note out of my purse. Luckily, I had even brought notes. They were something I seldom carried around these days. I was going to hand it to Madam Lee when she told me to leave it on the silver dish in the centre of the table.

I left my money on the dish, and Madam Lee covered it with a silky purple fabric. My ears pricked; I could hear Jess talking to someone outside. All the red curtains inside the van were closed, so I couldn't see who she was talking with, but I thought I heard Gary's voice.

"Now, shall we start with your palm?" Madam Lee asked.

"Does it matter which one?"

"Let's start with the right hand."

I presented my right hand to her. Madam Lee only took hold of my hand briefly before dropping it. Her face, which was peaches and cream before, turned white. "I'm going to have to stop your reading," she said. She swiped the fabric off the dish and handed me back my money.

"Why?" My own heart was drumming as fast as hers was if the pulse in her neck was anything to go by. "Did you see something?"

"I'm not feeling great," Madam Lee said. She stood up and pressed a hand to her stomach. "Upset tummy. It happens to me sometimes."

I stared her down like Mam did when she was trying to suss if I was lying, but Madam Lee wouldn't look at me.

"Okay." I stood up. I wanted to ask her again if she had seen anything, but maybe it was better not knowing with the way that she had reacted. I opened the door and walked out. I heard it lock a few seconds later.

Jess was leaning against a railing, taking another drink

from her flask—I'll give it to her; she was truly bold. "You're never done that fast?"

"I'm not. We didn't even get started. Well, we sort of did, but then she freaked out and ended the reading by saying that she had an upset tummy." I looked at the caravan, expecting to see Madam Lee peeking out of the curtains but they were still.

"Really? That's pretty weird."

"You think she saw something?"

"No," Jess said, but the tone in her voice suggested otherwise. Strange of her to even attempt to calm me. I bet inside she was delighted.

"You do, don't you?" I felt sick now thinking of what Madam Lee could've seen to give her such a reaction.

Jess pointed to the food stalls on the promenade. "Look around you; any one of these could've given Madam Lee her dose. Not your future, which I know is going to be dazzling. You're going to get a part in Ben's Hamlet play—"

"Macbeth," I said.

Jess shrugged. She was no theatre connoisseur. "And you'll kill at that. Then you'll finish your degree and become a big mad actor. But before any of that happens, the two of us are going to get slaughtered and have a wild night."

I smiled— her little spiel had cheered me up. Regardless of if she didn't believe it, I did. My future was rosy, and I knew that, but there was still a sick feeling in the pit of my stomach. Maybe there was a stomach bug going around. There was always something, wasn't there?

Jess tilted her flask my way. "Want some?"

"A proper drink in the pub," I said. "If I drank anymore of that, I'll be as sick as your one in there." I looked at the caravan again; this time, I could see the telltale twitch of the curtain. My stomach felt like someone was squeezing it with a gigantic fist. "She's looking at us," I whispered.

"Who is?" Jess asked. She was used to people looking at her with her loud hair and louder jewellery.

"Madam Lee: palm reader with the upset stomach or knowledge of my dark and twisted future. For my sake, I hope it's the former."

"No, she isn't," Jess said.

The curtains were still again. "Well, she was," I said. "The curtains weren't moving by themselves."

Jess put her arm around my shoulder and led me onto the promenade. "She was probably looking at how impossibly cool I am. Now, why don't we get you some food and then join Gary and Ben in the pub? I was talking with the two of them when you were inside. They told us to join them in the Black Horse."

Once again, I let Jess lead the way. I held onto my crumpled €20 and only released it while paying for my chocolate doughnut. It wasn't much food, but it would have to suffice to line my stomach. I was still eating it when we arrived at the Black Horse. The outside of the ancient pub was black as usual, but the horse silhouette above the door had recently been painted gold.

There was a bouncer outside the door counting the number of people that entered the premises. Jess and myself were the last two that he let in before people had to queue. Inside, the pub was packed. Jess grabbed my hand and squeezed. She led me away from the ground floor down steep wooden steps that brought us to the lower level. There was a band setting up on a small stage, and people were laughing and drinking on the dance floor. At the back of the section were tables and chairs, and every seat was taken. Here, there was another bar area with a queue in front. Another tug on my hand and we were outside. To the right was a bar that specialised in cocktails. I saw a woman with straight blonde hair pouring a pink drink from a silver jug into a glass. Maybe tonight, I'd have to forgo my usual cider for something different.

"I think I see them," Jess said.

She was right. Jess had great sight with her big eyes. She could spot people from far away. To the left was a large seating area. Jess pulled me through it until we arrived at Ben and Gary's table.

"Lacey Lou," Gary said. If his smile were any wider, he'd crack his face. "Ye did make it. I was hoping ye would."

"Don't call me Lacey Lou," I said. Louise is my middle name. I wasn't a fan of it. Gary only knew it because our lecturer had called me that at the start of first year.

"Sorry," Gary said. "We kept ye seats." He showcased the seats like they were a sought-after prize.

I sat down. "Thanks," I said. There was no sign of Ben, but a half-finished pint of Guinness was in front of an empty chair. "Ye here long?"

"Not long before ye. We got the last table." He smiled again—Gary seemed to be forever smiling. He'd make a great Joker.

Jess took off her leather jacket and put it on the back of

her seat. "I'll get us drinks," she said. "Cider for you?"

She knew my usual tipple. "I'll be as wild as you and get a cocktail," I said. "And I don't mind which one; you can surprise me."

Jess was delighted with my answer and walked away, beaming as happily as Gary. I watched her disappear into the mass of people.

She was gone for ten minutes when Ben arrived. I had only just spotted him talking to a woman with bright pink hair. I guess Jess was right about him being like Byron.

"Lacey." Here was another one happy to see me. "I was hoping that you'd join us."

"You want to ask me about the auditions again?"

"I do indeed," Ben said.

"When is it that they start?" I asked.

"Next week."

Jess placed a Long Island Iced Tea before me. "To fulfil your tea craving."

I took a drink. "It's good. Thanks for getting it. The next one is on me." I raised my glass. "Cheers." We clinked our matching drinks together.

"You're a witch, I hear?" Ben asked Jess.

"Gary has been telling you all about me then," Jess said.

"He loves to tell anyone who will listen, don't you?"

"Same way as you love telling everyone about yourself," Gary said.

"I am, anyway," Jess said. She drank from her drink. Not a dainty sip. Everything was large in life for Jess.

"How are you a witch?" Ben asked. "Do you've magic powers or something?"

"Yes, I do," Jess said. "And yes, I can turn you into a frog before you ask."

"I was just about to ask," Ben said. "You must be a witch then if you can read my mind."

Jess rolled her eyes. If she wasn't content sitting there drinking, I knew she would've gone home. But the drinks were good. Even better, I'd say they were great. We finished our first one and then the next. Soon, there was a pile of glasses on the table that the young fella collecting glasses couldn't keep clear for long.

"You can't really think you are a witch though," Ben asked. "I mean, it's all nonsense, isn't it?" He was tripping and slurring all over his words. I could tell that even if I was travelling on the same road as him. Only I hadn't made quite the same distance. He didn't let Jess answer before his eyes were on mine. "What about you, Lacey? Are you a witch too?"

I laughed. "Of course, I'm not."

"But you're interested in the same things as her," he nodded his head at Jess. "If you were in getting your fortune told."

"*Her* has a name," Jess said. "And lots of people get their fortune told."

Ben grinned. "Now you really will put a spell on me."

It was here that my memory deserted me. I'll tell you what I do remember. I got another drink. Cider this time— the cocktails were double the price, and funds were getting uncomfortably low. I remember wobbling my way over to the bathroom and rushing out when I heard the first fireworks go off. I remember going over to the crowd of people, all of them stary-eyed and in temporary peace. I was among them. I didn't care I was squashed among strangers. Not at all. Then it was over. I went back to the table where we had been sitting. The only thing remaining were two empty lipstick-stained glasses. Even Jess's leather coat was no longer on the back of the seat.

I searched the Black Horse for the three, starting downstairs and then inside, where the band played to dancing bodies. They were not on the ground floor either.

I went into the bathroom and rang Jess's phone—fifteen times, according to my call log. She didn't answer any of my calls.

At some point, I gave up and went to the bus stop. The bus driver was about to leave when I arrived.

"Lucky you," he told me. "You'd be stuck here for the night, sleeping on the beach."

"Lucky me," I said. "Lucky me." And that's all that I remember.

.

August 26th

I woke to a pounding headache and a mouth that felt as if it had been stuffed with cotton. When my eyes creaked open, they were met with the sight of the rain pelting against the window. It wasn't bright, not a bit, yet the light was too intense for my headache. Not having the strength to close the curtains, I slid under the duvet and listened to the rain from my cocoon. I pushed my hands over my ears, but the sound of the water escaped into my eardrum. I squeezed the tips of my forefingers against my ears; this replaced the sound of the rain with the flow of my blood as it moved through my body. I wished I had my headphones. I wished I didn't have to be reminded of my life. Not that I wanted it to end; I love being alive. It's the preciousness of life that I hate. My heart pounded.

Mam was downstairs in the kitchen, sporadically banging drawers and kitchen equipment. This meant one thing: she was angry. The kitchen door slammed, and footsteps pounded up the stairs. Mam flung open the door and snarled when she saw me balled up in bed.

"I know you're awake, Lacey. Don't pretend that you're asleep. There'll be no going easy on you today, even if the head is pounding off you."

"You saw me then."

"Course I saw you; the whole bloody town saw you; you were in some awful condition, so you were."

"I'm a grown woman, and I'm allowed to have a few drinks if I want to."

"That may be true, but as long as you're staying in this house, I don't want to see you coming here scuttered like you were last night. Have I made myself clear?"

"Fine," I said.

"You stay away from that Jess one. If you hadn't been with her, you wouldn't have been in that condition."

I didn't say anything further. I just stared at Mam. She hated it when I did that. She said it made her feel like she was someone in a freak show.

"Do something with the state of this room, will you?" She saw the little goddess statue that Jess had given me two weeks ago. Which goddess it was, I couldn't tell. "And get rid of that pagan devil worshipper." Mam left, slamming the door behind her.

I didn't know if Mam meant the statue or Jess herself. Probably both. I wasn't feeling too delighted with Jess at that moment either, I can tell you. It wasn't the first time that we lost each other when we were drinking, but we didn't just lose each other; she had ditched me. Despite my drunken state last night, I had put my phone in its usual place on the blocked-up fireplace on the opposite side of the room. It vibrated. The sound was loud against the wood. I left my warm bed. The pain in my head was sharp when I stood up and sharper with each step that I took. Jess's picture filled the screen.

There was a minute when I debated answering the phone, but my curiosity won. "Hello?"

"Lacey," Jess said. She sounded relieved. "Where the hell did you go?" There was no relief now, just anger.

"Where did I go? You were the one that ditched me."

"I ditched you?" Jess laughed. "I spent all night looking for you. The three of us did."

"No. I went to the toilet. I was looking at the fireworks, and then when I returned to the table, the three of ye were gone."

"Because we were looking for you. Someone told Ben that they saw you leaving, so we went searching."

"I only left after I couldn't find ye," I said.

Jess laughed. "I guess we were all just in the horrors then."

"Maybe," I said icily.

"We called to your parents' house, and your mother told me to fuck off. That's how I knew you were home because if you weren't, your mother would've been pestering me with questions."

"I rang you, too," I said. The ice was thawing in my voice.

"I know," Jess said. "I was kicking myself for missing the calls."

Mam was banging downstairs once again.

"What's all that noise?" Jess asked. "You back on the session again?"

"My mother. She's not impressed with me coming home in the horrors."

"Your mother isn't impressed with anything. I suppose

there's no hope of me calling around later? She'd probably hit me over the head with something."

"I'll meet you in the park." I checked the time on my Fitbit. It was midday. "Meet me there at three?"

"Sounds good," Jess said.

We hung up. I checked my phone. There were fifty-six missed calls from Jess. With the first one at 10. p.m. and the last one at 3.46.a.m. I guess she hadn't ditched me. But I was still annoyed at her and myself. I shouldn't have drunk so much, and she shouldn't have been feeding me drink, knowing what a lightweight I was. But Jess didn't care, as long as she had someone to drink with. It was always the same with her.

I went back to bed for another hour. When I woke up, it was half past one, and my headache was gone. There was dead quiet in the house, which could only mean that Mam wasn't at home. That was good. The headache might've gone, but I was still wicked hungover. Dealing with Mam on a normal day was bad enough, never mind with a hangover.

I showered, dressed, and managed to eat toast. Dad arrived home when I was on my second slice. I saw him peeking into the sitting room to see if Mam was there.

There was a look of relief when he saw that her chair was empty.

"She's not here, Dad," I said. "She's run away to join a nunnery."

Dad came into the kitchen. He was wearing his brown suit with a matching brown tie. "Lacey," he said. "You were in an awful way last night. I thought your mother's heart was set to collapse when she saw the cut of you."

"Sorry," I said.

"No need to be sorry. Just be careful."

He was on a late lunch. I had a cup of tea with him, and then I went to meet Jess in the park. The park was a fifteen-minute walk from my house. The rain had cleared, but the weather was still grey. From inside, it looked cold, but after ten minutes of walking, I had to take off my coat and drape it over my arm with the heat coming out of me—of course, that could've been the hangover too. I passed under the archway that said St. Enda's Park and walked on the path to the benches. There were three of them near enough to each other but with enough space between each to give you privacy. It was here that Jess and I often met for chats. If the seats were in use, then we'd sit on the grass, but they weren't taken. There was only one person there: Jess. She sat on the middle bench. Her eyes were on the tree above her.

"The leaves are starting to change," she said when she saw me. She was pale and looked worse than I did. I bet while she was searching for me, she stayed on the drink.

"You don't look great," I said. I kept to the opposite side of the bench, my eyes on the soggy grass.

"Are you annoyed at me? It really was just all of us being drunken eejits and losing each other. Gary ended up getting lost too. We found him at the bus stop. He said he went there in case you showed up."

"Is that why you wanted to see me? You could've told me that over the phone."

"I wanted to see you. To talk to you," Jess yawned. She was wearing a purple coat the same shade as the bags under her eyes. "Sorry. I got an hour's sleep if I got any."

"You weren't just staying up getting drunk?"

Jess shook her head. "No, Mammy, I wasn't."

I had to laugh at that. I did sound like my mother. "So, why couldn't you sleep?"

"Worried about you for ages. Then I was thinking about going to Cork and finishing my degree there."

We had been here before. Jess was originally from

Cork. Every so often, she talked about transferring. I couldn't see why she was so keen on this when she only had one person that she knew living there. Just about everybody else had abandoned her. "Will you go, Jess?"

"Maybe. But will I tell you where I am going for definite?"

"Home to get some sleep?" I asked.

"I'm going to do a little full moon ritual in the woods near the river. I know it's not the full moon anymore, but the energy will still be there. You want to join in with me?"

I didn't have to think twice. "No."

"Didn't you say that you'd like to join me for a ritual?" Jess asked.

I could feel her pulling me to look at her. I did. "It's all a bit weird, though, isn't it? All this moon ritual stuff."

"I don't think so," Jess said. "It's really beautiful."

"I'll let you do your beautiful ritual. The only thing I want to do is get home and start reading Macbeth. The auditions are on next week. I had a text from Ben to remind me."

"He texted you?" Jess asked.

"Yes. Gary did, too. They confirmed your story about losing me." I stood up. I'd had enough of the park and the grey day.

"I wasn't lying," Jess shouted. I wasn't expecting it, so I jumped. "I never lie."

"Don't get yourself into a heap," I said. Jess's face was all red. It did this whenever she was angry. "I wasn't accusing you of lying."

Jess took out her crumpled cigarette box and pulled out a cigarette. She was the only person I knew who still smoked cigarettes; everyone else was on the rollies or vapes. She lit it and inhaled. "Sorry for snapping. I'm just wrecked."

"Leave your ritual and go home to bed. You'd be better off." I started walking when Jess called me back.

"Lacey?"

I turned around.

"You're still my friend, aren't you?"

I had to think about it for a beat. We were different, Jess and myself. I knew that, but differences could make things work. "I'm still your friend," I said. I even smiled at her. Jess seemed satisfied with that.

When I got home, Mam was in the kitchen. The windows were all fogged up with her cooking without the extractor fan on. I was only in the door when she turned to me.

"You were with her. I saw the two of ye in Enda's sitting on the bench like two winos." Mam had a knife in her hand, and she slashed it through a carrot.

"I didn't see you in Enda's," I said.

"You wouldn't cause you were staring at the grass like you were stoned out of your head. And I'd say you were, too. That Jess one is probably growing weed in that little shithole of a flat she rents. I have a mind to ring the guards on that one." Mam picked up the knife again and waved it in the air. "I told her last night to stay away from you."

"So, she did call here last night then."

"Oh, she did, looking out of her mind. The eyes on her nearly falling out her skull." Back to the carrot, Mam sliced through it hard enough to leave cuts on the board.

"Why do you hate her so much?" I asked. Mam had never taken to Jess. I had never even told her about Jess going off with that young fella I'd the crush on. But that month when I didn't speak to Jess, Mam had been delighted.

"She's just bad," Mam said. She wasn't even shouting now. She said it calmly. I think that's what frightened me. "She makes me feel scared for you."

Jess and her intensity had scared me. Sometimes, I felt like she wanted to combust and bring me along with her. I poured myself a glass of water and drank half of it back. Her eyes scared me, too. They were just too knowing. Too seeing. "Can I help you with the dinner?"

Mam nodded. "That would be nice, Lacey."

I peeled the potatoes. I was careful not to nip my fingers. I'd done it before, and it had stung much worse than it looked.

"I only want to protect you," Mam said.

"I know," I said.

I opened the window, letting all the steam out of the kitchen. We didn't talk about Jess again, and I didn't answer her call when she rang me that evening. I was busy reading Macbeth.

August 27th

I didn't sleep well. I dreamt that the moon was covered by a dense fog. I sat alone in the woods, waiting for Jess to appear. When Jess did show up, she was soaked in a liquid I couldn't discern. She hugged me, leaving my white clothes red. That's when I knew she was soaked in blood. I screamed, and Jess shushed me. My lips stuck together. I tried to pry them open, but they wouldn't budge. Jess walked over to a large cast iron cauldron. Mid-stir, she looked up at the moon and howled. At the howl, a dozen hooded figures emerged from the shadows, all holding a candle in thin hands. I tried to run away and only managed a few feet before they dragged me back. The figures pulled down their hoods; all of them had Mam's face. It wasn't seeing Mam's face that caused me the terror; it was Jess's absolute disinterest in my fear.

I left my bed. The sheets were tousled and damp.

There were only a few days left before college started again. For the summer, I had been minding two children living nearby, but their mother was on holiday now and didn't need me. It was a good job. Easy money. I had been excited about having these last days off to laze around before the rush began. I opened the curtains to the sun blaring. I pressed my hand against the glass—it was warm. It wasn't a day for staying inside. It was a day for ice cream and strolling along the seaside.

Throughout the summer, when I wasn't working, I'd hang around with Jess. We had our beach days and our days walking through the woods. They were good times, but I didn't feel like seeing Jess today. I'd have myself for company instead. I might as well enjoy the last few days of solitude while I still had it.

Mam was outside hanging up the washing when I left the house. She was wearing her yellow blouse—I knew she was in a good mood as she always wore yellow when she was happy.

"Good morning," I said.

Mam turned around. She was all smiles until she saw that I was dressed and ready to head off. "Where are you going?" she asked.

"I'm going to get some sea air. It would do me the world of good."

"Who are you going with?" She took a soaking-wet T-shirt from the basket. The T-shirt was red and reminded me of Jess's blood-soaked attire from my dream.

"Just by myself. I said I better make use of the day before I'm back to college."

"Have a good day, then." Mam was back to smiling. She knew when I was telling her the truth.

I left the house and walked to the bus stop. It was a soft morning with few cars out. I only had to wait a few minutes before the bus came along. Only a couple of people were on board. All of them, like me, were on their own. When we arrived at Moonbay East, I thanked the driver and left the bus.

It was, owing to the sea air, a little breezier than it had been in town. But it was the nice, warm type of breeze that felt refreshing rather than windy. Now I was here, I wasn't quite sure what to do. I missed Jess for her decision-making. It was silly really. I was perfectly capable of making my own choices in life. I couldn't have that mentality anymore. I inhaled the sea air. I would read Macbeth and learn my lines. I had packed it for that purpose. I walked to the promenade. Gone were the food vendors and the hordes of people. Gone too was Madam Lee and her little caravan. I hadn't thought about her until I saw her caravan missing from the car park.

"Lacey!" A young woman with a chin-length brown bob ran towards me. She held an ice cream in one hand, which she almost dropped in excitement.

"Hi, Evie." Evie studied Theatre too, and she was an endless ball of energy. Jess told me once that Evie sucked up other people's energy and used it for herself, and that's why people felt so exhausted when they were around her.

She wrapped her arms around me, pressing her ice cream into the top of my jacket. She saw what she had done and rubbed the ice cream away. "Sorry about that. I was just so happy to see you. How has your summer been? Has it been great?"

"It has," I said. "Yours?"

"Amazing. But I can't wait to get back. Imagine we are going into our last year. It's just so exciting." Evie did her usual little Evie jump up and down.

I smiled at her. I couldn't help it. She was like an irritating but lovable puppy.

"You've got coffee, I see. I've just drunk a large latte. I'd have more, but I'm going to get a reading done from this lady called Madam Lee. She's meant to be absolutely wonderful." Evie pulled my Fitbit towards her and checked the time. "And I must run, or I'll be late."

"Madam Lee? Seventh daughter of a seventh daughter?"

"That's the one." Evie was still holding my watch, and I could feel the heat of her hand on my skin. "You know who she is!"

"Where is she?"

"Parked down there." She pointed to the very end of the promenade towards a car park near the dunes. She let go of my hand and hugged me once again. "I'll see you super soon. Have a lovely day!"

"Bye, Evie," I said. I could see her running as I walked along the promenade myself. I wondered what Madam Lee would tell Evie.

Although the promenade was populated with easy Sunday strollers and the rides were in motion in the park opposite, it was quiet. It was easy for me to see Evie until she walked out of my eyeline. I continued walking; any hope of sitting on the beach and reading had gone. There was a new mission. I needed to talk to Madam Lee again.

The sign in front of Madam Lee's caravan swung in the gentle breeze. I walked right past and could hear Evie's laughter inside. No fear of Madam Lee having an upset stomach today. I waited across the road, standing next to a Mini Cooper that was in need of a wash. Here, I put my Macbeth to use and stared at it while I drank my coffee. I had finished it and was holding onto the empty cup for a good ten minutes when Evie came laughing her way out of the van.

"I always knew my future was going to be good. But just hearing you say it gives me no end of relief." Evie had her hand over her heart and that never-ending smile on her face. She leaned into Madam Lee and said something softly enough that I couldn't make it out. An air kiss later, and Evie was on her way.

I caught Madam Lee just as she was stepping into her van. "Excuse me, are you available for a reading?"

Madam Lee was about to say "yes." She had started

saying the y sound and abruptly stopped when she saw it was me standing there. "I'm actually on my lunch break."

"You were just about to say yes. I know that you were. Which only makes me believe that you saw something the other day. And I'd really like to know what that was." This was a new Lacey. Not the woman who needed someone to make constant decisions for her but the one who was capable of just about anything. "Please tell me."

Madam Lee walked into the van. "Come in," she said. I wasn't expecting that. I thought I'd have to plead with her for longer.

The van still smelled like chai tea and cinnamon. Madam Lee sat down as before, and I joined on the opposite seat. Her huge gold earrings jangled when she moved her head. "I am sorry for kicking you out before."

"Did you see something?" I asked.

Madam Lee nodded.

"What did you see?"

"Are you sure that you want to know? Mostly, people come to me wanting the good news. I give it to them, and that makes them very happy. They rarely want to know the truth."

It was my turn to nod.

"Darkness and decay," Madam Lee said. "The latter truly did make me feel sick."

"Darkness and decay?" I whispered.

"It surrounds you."

"You can tell that now with me just sitting here?"

Madam Lee's earrings shook with her head. "Sometimes, the feelings come strong. Other times, there is nothing. Now, I can only see a young lady sitting before me."

"What else? Do you see more?" There was raw panic in my voice. It scared me hearing it there.

Madam Lee's finger ran across my palm before she grabbed my hand. A jolt of electricity ran along my arm and seeped into the bones. I tried to pull my hand away, but Madam Lee's grasp tightened. She let out a groan and dropped my hand.

"What the hell was that about?" I asked.

"You wanted to know more," she said.

"And you'll tell more by breaking my hand?" I cradled my hand. Red marks had dented the skin like an angry tattoo. The area that wasn't red was cold and white.

"The messages come for me through touch. That's how my gift works. If you want to call it a gift." She shook her head. "It's not always. For you, it is."

"Because you almost broke the hand off me?"

"There is a different road that you can travel."

The pain didn't seem so important anymore. "How?" I asked, leaning closer to Madam Lee. There were flecks of gold in her green eyes.

"Stay away from three witches."

"Stay away from three witches?" I repeated.

Madam Lee nodded. "That's the message that came through. Does it make any sense to you?"

I tilted my head. There was every possibility that Madam Lee was having me on, but why would she be? The silver dish was still to the side of the table, but she hadn't asked me to drop a cent into it. Not to mention her extreme reaction the last time we met and her unhappiness at seeing me again. "No," I said. But I had spoken too soon. I reached for the water bottle in my bag and found Macbeth. "The Weird Sisters. There are three witches in Macbeth. I was going to audition for it. Could that be it—the three witches?"

"I don't know," Madam Lee said softly. "I just get the messages. But I can't deny the connection between the two of them." Her face looked as pale as my hand, and there was a glaze of sweat on her forehead.

"So, I shouldn't audition?" I asked.

"It's your call," Madam Lee said. She fanned her hand in front of her face. "I'd offer to do you a tarot reading for clarity, but when I get messages, they drain me of all my energy. I'm going to have to take a little nap and then make use of the ocean to recharge my batteries. If you want to come back later, I can read for you then."

I didn't want to come back later. I didn't ever want to see Madam Lee again. She had given me her message, and that was enough for me. There would be plenty of other plays. There was no need to take the risk. "No thank you," I said. "There can't be anything else that message can mean."

"I'm sure you're right," she said. "It's too strong of a connection."

I stood up. And just before leaving the van, I asked: "Where do these messages come from? Are they from a good or an evil place?"

Madam Lee shrugged. "They come from somewhere. Take care of yourself now, Lacey, and try to enjoy your final year of college."

I thanked her and left the van. Only walking back to the

bus stop did I consider that I hadn't told her my name or that I was in college. Maybe she heard Jess call my name, or maybe Evie had described me. Or perhaps she just knew. I'd take the latter and add it as further reasoning as to why I couldn't audition for Macbeth.

September 18th

The first two weeks of college sped by. Each morning, I cycled to C.T.U., passing the cars that were lined along the road bumper to bumper. The leaves had started changing colour in August, and some of the eager ones had fallen from the branches. However, the weather hadn't become autumnal in the least. It was warm for Ireland, and my classmates and myself would sit out on the grass during our free time between classes. They were an easy two weeks and enjoyable ones. It was good to catch up with everyone and hear about their summers.

On Friday, the first chilly day of September, two assignments were announced. Not only that, but talk of our final third-year performance began. I was nervous, but I was also wicked excited. My classmates weren't that bothered. I suppose it was because they were all hung up on the Macbeth auditions that were starting that week. And I, now can you believe this, was the only one out of the ten of us who wasn't going to audition. Not that it was from a lack of trying on Ben's part. When I told him I wasn't interested, he was on the phone begging me to audition, telling me I was his vision of what Lady Macbeth should be. It was very flattering, but I still had to stick with my decision and decline the audition.

Now, it was Monday morning, and again, the weather was chilly. Chillier than it had been on Friday. I locked my bike at the back of campus and walked to the Arts Building. Celtic Technological University was no fan of the arts—it was the least loved out of all the buildings, with walls that needed painting and carpets that were mostly thread. When it rained, the ceilings often leaked, and sometimes the toilets were out of service, and we'd have to walk to a different building to use them there. My class, the Theatre Studies majors were only in this building twice a week. Our practical classes were held in a hall in a different part of campus, a twenty-minute walk away.

Natalie, probably the only woman in my year who could

incite feelings of jealousy from me, was walking ahead. Her glossy brown hair swished from side to side. I wasn't jealous of her hair; I liked my hair. It wasn't poker straight like Nat's, but it held a wave. I wasn't jealous that almost everyone, male and female, seemed to have a crush on her. I was jealous because Natalie was brilliant. I hate admitting that, but there you have it. Beautiful Natalie was a brilliant actor. If I'm truly honest, I think she was even better than I was.

She saw me coming and held the door open. She didn't smile. Natalie rarely smiled.

"You're auditioning for Macbeth, I take it?" Natalie asked. She wasn't originally from Ireland, but she had been living here since she was four, and there was just a trace of her accent left. I couldn't even tell you where she had been living before—just somewhere in mainland Europe.

"No," I said. "I want to focus on the final year."

Natalie blinked. It was the slow type that seemed to speak a hundred words. None of them were impressed.

"Lacey." I knew the voice well. I'd been avoiding it as much as possible for the past few weeks. I turned around, and there was Jess. She was wearing gothy boots that reached to her knees and a hot pink coat. We had only hung out once since the meeting in the park. Like now, we had met in the hallway, and she had pleaded with me to join her for coffee until I relented. That time, she had brought out her tarot cards and attempted to give me a reading in the middle of the coffee shop before I told her to put the cards away.

"Since when are you afraid of the tarot?" she had asked.

"I'm not afraid of it," I said. It was true. It was Jess who scared me. Ever since that night I had dreamed about her and her blood-soaked gown, I wanted to be as far away from her as possible. And I certainly didn't want her to have the knowledge that the tarot cards could give.

"Where have you been?" Jess asked. She was skinnier and paler if such a thing were possible. Forget about a witch; Jess was morphing into a skeleton.

"Around," I said.

"How are you?" Jess asked. She was trying to sound carefree—I could tell she wasn't in the way that her voice was too high-pitched.

"Good," I said. "You?"

"Peachy," Jess said. She coughed. "If the peach were decaying."

Natalie, who had been filling up her bottle at the water

fountain, strolled over to us. "Thank you for the reading. It was most insightful." Then Natalie did something that I rarely saw her do: she smiled.

"You're very welcome," Jess said.

"You are coming to Marcus's party?"

Marcus was another Theatre Studies student. He was good but nowhere near Natalie or myself. It was his birthday on Saturday, and he had spoken of little else since the start of term.

"I will," Jess said.

"And you will bring your board?" Natalie asked.

"What board is this?" I asked.

"My Ouija board," Jess said. "Bought it last week."

My stomach dropped. "You're not serious? You shouldn't be playing around with that stuff."

"You've turned into your mother," Jess laughed.

"No, I haven't," I said a little too harshly.

Marcus rushed past us. He had overdone the cologne.

"Goodbye, Jess," Natalie said. "Bring your board."

"I will," Jess said. Just for a moment, she didn't look so skeletal, and then, as soon as Natalie left, she was back looking deflated. "I didn't mean anything by saying you're turning into your mother; I just find it funny that anyone would be afraid of a Ouija board."

"People are afraid of all different things," I said. It was true, and I wouldn't laugh at someone just because they're not into spiders.

"Are you going to Marcus's party?" she asked.

"I am," I said. Then, because maybe I had been giving Jess a hard time, I added, "I guess we could walk there together?"

"That would be great," Jess said. "Will we meet at the park?"

I nodded. "Well, I better get moving."

We said goodbye. I heard Jess's heavy boots hit against the floor as she walked away.

September 23rd

Natalie was going to be Lady Macbeth. She strolled into class on Thursday morning and announced it to us all. Our lecturer was ever so delighted for her. I wasn't. Even though I had resigned myself to the fact that I wouldn't be in the play, I was still not impressed. Yes, I was jealous, and I've no trouble admitting that. But I wasn't the only jealous one, judging by all the dirty looks sent Natalie's way. I wonder how Natalie would feel if she knew that I was Ben's first choice for the part. Sure, he had practically begged me to be Lady Macbeth. I wouldn't say that to her though. Let her have her moment. Or let her have another moment.

I rid myself of thoughts of Natalie as I got ready for the

party. I was looking forward to it. My excitement might have been bigger because I knew Ben was going to be there.

Jess waited for me at the entrance to the park. She was wearing purple boots with an impossibly high heel. Her black skirt just covered her butt cheeks, and her leather jacket had a nodge burn in the sleeve. She had a shopping bag in one hand and a cigarette in the other. I had a feeling what was in the shopping bag and it wasn't alcohol. The drink would be in her handbag.

"It's good to see you," Jess said. She hugged me. I could feel her bones sticking into me. "I've missed hanging out with you." Those shadows were still under her eyes. I had never seen her looking as bad.

"You enjoying being back at college?" I asked.

"It's okay," Jess said. "Probably what I like about it the most is that it's our final year."

Marcus lived in a house along with three other students about a twenty-minute walk away. We had been there last year at a random session at the end of a night out. Natalie had been there too. I couldn't recall Jess and her being the best of friends then.

"How did you and Natalie get to be such great friends?"
I asked.

"I'm designing and making a costume for one of my
assignments. I put up a poster looking for a model, and
Natalie got back to me. Turns out she's really into costume
design herself."

I stopped listening. It was a skill I learned from living
with my mother; I could almost completely drown out
someone when they were speaking. We walked through
town. Jess kept pace with my fast footsteps almost too
easily. I had to wonder if her feet weren't regular and had
the same type of arches as Barbie's.

"Have you?" Jess asked. She had put on lashings of
mascara, making her already humongous eyes extra bug-
like and glaring.

"Have I what?" I asked. That was the trouble with
zoning out: it was difficult to know when to zone back in."

"Wasn't Ben mad to get you to play Lady Macbeth?
Then I hear that Natalie has got the role?"

"I want to put my full attention on the final year. It's too
important, and I don't want to spread myself thin," I said.
We were on the outskirts of town now, on Kevin's Street.
Sometimes, I came this way on my cycle to college, but I

hadn't in over a week. And in that week, the green in front of the housing estate that we were currently passing had become smothered in yellow, orange, and red leaves.

"I think that's a good decision." She took out her pentagram flask and drank. "Want some?" she asked, pointing the flask at me.

"No," I said. I was brought back to the night of the fireworks. I wondered if we'd split up again tonight. If we did, I wouldn't care.

Jess screwed the lid back onto the flask with her long, thin fingers. The ends of which were like claws with the nails pointed and red the way that she had them. When I was a child at Halloween, they sold rubber witch's fingers that you would put over your own. They looked exactly like Jess's.

Evie was sitting on the step outside of Marcus's house, eating a slice of pizza. When she saw us approach, she placed the pizza box down on the step and wrapped her arms around me. "I'm so happy to see ye," she said.

Evie had cut her hair, and it was now in a pixie cut. It suited her, making her look more like an elf than the Weird Sister she had been cast as. "It's always great to see you too, Evie," I said.

"Did you bring the Ouija board?" She asked Jess. "I've always wanted to try one of them."

Jess held up the shopping bag. "I did."

Evie clapped her hands. "That's brilliant. Would you guys like some pizza? I've got lots of pizza?" She ran over to the step, retrieved the box, and pointed it at us.

"I'm okay," Jess said. "I haven't been able to eat much. My stomach is wicked nauseous. Final year nerves kicking in, I guess."

We left Evie sitting on the step, holding her box of pizza.

"What's she on?" Jess whispered. "Did you see the size of her pupils? They were bigger than the universe."

Ben came out of a doorway to the left with a beer in his hand. "She's on bangers. You're a loud whisperer," he said to Jess. "Very loud."

Inside the room Ben came out of, several people were playing a game of cards and drinking. Old-school rock and roll poured from a tiny speaker on the mantle. I could see Natalie drinking a glass of white wine—unusual for Natalie, who rarely drank alcohol.

Jess walked off and went into the kitchen. Her heels

click-clacked on the tiles. She was like a ghost in a story, making their presence known with chains, except Jess's chains, were her choice of footwear.

"Not going to lie, I bawled my eyes out when you didn't audition," Ben said.

"I'm sure you did," I said.

"I did. I've been drinking myself into a stupor." He held up his beer can.

"Wouldn't you be drinking something a little stronger to get into a stupor?" I asked.

"I may not be drinking something stronger, but I've got something stronger." He pulled out a baggie from his jeans pocket and showed it to me. There were five tablets inside of it. "Bought them from the pixie outside. Would you like one?" He moved a tablet to the top of the bag and expected me to say yes until he saw the look on my face. "Only if you want one, that is?"

Time went funny the way it does when you've to make a large decision. It was silly because it wasn't even a big deal. "They're not too strong, are they?"

"Not at all," he said.

I took the tablet. It left a chalky residue on my sweaty palm. Before I could chicken out, I swallowed it, grabbing

Ben's beer to wash it down.

"They're not strong unless it's your first time taking pills," he said.

"What?"

"I'm just joking." Ben placed his hands on mine and looked me in the eye. "You're okay. You're going to have a great night." When he did that eyebrow raise thing, my heart spun.

And I was okay. Soon enough, after that initial nervousness had passed, I felt great. Ben and myself left the hallway, went into the kitchen, and spent the next while tucked away in a corner, talking about nothing and everything.

"Hey, Lacey Lou." It was the smiling Gary. "I heard you didn't audition for Macbeth. You've left poor Ben only heartbroken."

"He's told me," I said.

Gary moved in closer, breaking the bubble between Ben and myself. "I hear your one Jess has a Ouija board. Back to her witchy crap again."

I had forgotten about Jess while speaking with Ben. I didn't even know where she had gone.

"She and Natalie are one step away from flying off on

their broomsticks. "You going to join them, are you, Lacey?"

"A Ouija board?" Ben asked. "I've never seen one of them in real life. Let's have a look then." He walked away, leaving me on my own with Gary before Evie appeared and grabbed my hand. I had never noticed before how tiny her hands were. I held one under my eyes. Her nails were green and sparkly, and there were little brown leaves drawn on them.

"Do you like them?" Evie asked. "I did them myself."

"They're beautiful," I said.

Evie pulled me through the sitting room. The Doors were playing. I couldn't even tell you what song it was, but I'd know Jim Morrison's voice anywhere. Behind the stereo was a large ornate mirror—it was far too nice for a student house. It was smudged with all manner of dirt, and someone had written Disco Pigs in the middle of it. It had to have been Marcus, for he was obsessed with the play and the film. I stopped in front of the mirror and saw my reflection. My dark blonde hair was longer than it had ever been, reaching almost to my waist.

It was scraggly, and soon I'd have to trim it. It was my eyes that I was really looking at; they looked like alien eyes. I touched my finger against the mirror.

Evie pulled my hand again, and we left the sitting room. I was happy because it was too crowded. Jess and Natalie were climbing the stairs. We followed them up, and Evie took the lead. The carpets were even worse than in the Arts Building. Here, they were covered in stains of various colours and in dire need of a vacuum.

On the landing, we followed the noise into a bedroom with its curtain closed. This room was the cleanest part of the house, with everything gleaming and in its place, bar the people sitting in a circle on the bed.

"I'm here joining your coven," Ben said, looking at me.

"I'm not a witch," I said.

"So, this is it." Evie jumped onto the bed and took her place next to Jess. She knocked her hand against the board as if testing what material it was made from. "It's smaller than I expected it would be."

"I'm glad you're talking to the board and not me," Gary said. He had followed us upstairs. "Be about the worst thing you could say." He laughed nervously.

"And it's purple. I love that it's purple," Evie said.

Course, Jess's board would have to be purple. She had an obsession with the colour. She had even painted the walls in the flat she shared with two other students purple. The landlord was less than impressed, especially with the job she had done of it. An artist she might be, but a painter she was not.

"Are you staying here with the witches?" Gary asked Ben.

There was a dressing table straight in front of me with a purple and orange lava lamp on the top of it. The glass was hot when I touched it, and I immediately pulled my hand away.

The door opened, and Marcus strolled into the room. He had short brown hair and a wonky nose that looked like it would fall off with a push. "So, there is a meeting going on in my room," he said. He saw the Ouija board on the bed. "Ye weren't messing then."

"I never joke when it comes to spirits," Jess drank from the pentagram flask in her hand and passed it over to Natalie, who downed it as though it would cure everything that was wrong with her life. Not that there could be much wrong when you're beautiful and brilliant.

Marcus put his arm around my shoulder. "Do you like my lava lamp?"

I did. It distracted me from what was happening on the

bed. "It's beautiful."

"I'll stay with the witches," Ben said.

"I'll let ye weirdoes to it," Gary said. "I've no wish to summon any demons." He left the room and closed the door behind him.

"You going to sit down, Lacey?" Ben asked me. He patted the place beside him on the bed. I joined him. It wouldn't be so bad. I was being silly. I had no trouble having my tarot cards read before. I'd even used a pendulum on a few occasions and nothing bad had happened to me.

"It's so pretty," Evie said. Her eyes met mine, and I recoiled. They were too dark. Demon dark. Jess doesn't believe in demons, but I think she's wrong there. I think demons do exist. I started to stand up. This was silly. I shouldn't be here. Then I immediately fell back onto the bed.

Ben's hand was on my thigh. "You okay, Lacey?"

My skin was warm, almost as hot as the lava lamp. There was a cold can of cider in my hand. I pressed it against my cheeks. "I'm fine," I said. "Just fine."

Marcus was on the bed now, too. His large forehead was sweaty.

Natalie still had Jess's flask in her hand. She finished what was left in it and dumped it onto the mattress. Jess picked it up and shook it. "You finished it?" she asked. "I just put a naggin into that."

"Sorry," Natalie said. Her eyes were watery and red. Her hand went to her mouth—no need for words to know what that meant. Natalie crawled from the bed and fell to the ground with a thump—nothing brilliant about her there. I attempted to help her, but she swatted me away.

Natalie allowed Jess to help her from the floor. Then they were gone from the room, and it was just the four of us.

"I've never seen her like that," Marcus said. "Didn't even know that Natalie drank."

Evie picked up the planchette on the board and looked in through the eyehole. "Everyone has to go a little mad sometimes, don't they?"

"You're mad all the time, Evie," Marcus said.

Evie giggled. I didn't like her then. I didn't like the way her hair was sticking up all over the place or her demonic-looking eyes. I think I've got a thing about eyes; I didn't like Jess's either, did I? I was just like that character in "The Tell-Tale Heart." Except I wouldn't kill anyone. I'd never do that.

"You okay?" Ben asked. He had soulful, doughy eyes. I liked them. The world would be a better place if more people had Ben's eyes.

I couldn't speak, but I nodded. Seeing Natalie like that wasn't fun. I'd always considered her the better actor, the prettier, and the most brilliant. Now, she would only be a drunk, moody mess on the floor.

The door opened, and Jess walked into the room. "She's gone home."

Marcus scratched his forehead. "Are we going to get started with this then?"

"Can I have the planchette?" Jess asked, sitting back on the bed. She took it from Evie with her claw-like hands. Then Jess's eyes were on me, and they made my stomach turn with the coldness in them. How could I never see it before? "You okay, Lacey?" she asked me. She touched me with one of her claws, and I swear the touch burnt. I hated to admit Mam was right about anything, but there was something wrong with Jess.

"I'm fine," I said. If Ben hadn't kicked my foot, I wouldn't have smiled, and Jess would've enquired further. "Just peachy."

Jess was happy with that, and she put the planchette on the board. I should've left, but I was afraid I'd dive to the floor like Natalie and become as unbrilliant as her. I'd stay. "Aren't you going to join in Lace?" Jess asked, staring at me. "Or has Mammy finally put the fear of God into you?"

I rolled my eyes but hovered my finger above the planchette. Then something happened: my finger stuck onto the plastic. I attempted to pull it away, but my body wouldn't listen to the screaming from my brain, and I could only stare as the planchette moved around the board. Jess was watching. I could feel it. Sure enough, when I looked up, she was smirking at me.

D. The first letter. Everyone but me said the letter aloud. Onto E.

"Who's moving it?" Marcus asked. "One of ye is moving it."

A. There was scratching somewhere in the room, like nails on wood. No one else heard it. T.

Evie was giggling; the sound was just as intrusive as the scratching. H.

"Death," Evie said. She was still giggling. "We're talking to death, are we?"

Jess hushed her. Even her big bug eyes looked scared.

The scratching sound was louder now. S.

"Deaths," Marcus said. "Now, whichever one of you is moving it, change it to something a little more cheerful. U.

There was something in the corner of the room. I could see it standing there. R.

"Death sur?" Jess said. "Death sure?"

No, that wasn't it. Another R came next. Scratching again. O. Had Gary come back? Was he the one doing all of the scratching? Was he the one standing in the corner? U. My neck ached. It was stiff as I lifted my head and gazed at the corner of the room.

"N," Ben said. "Death surroun?" D came next. "I could hear them all say the letter like a demented group of schoolchildren learning their ABCs. But my eyes were focused on the thing in the corner. It couldn't have been Gary. Not unless he was on stilts. This was too tall and slim. It wore a long black cloak that reached down to the ankles, showing a peep of black boots. The hood on the coat was up, so I couldn't see the hair, nor could I see the face, which was completely concealed by a red mask with a bird-like beak where its nose should be. The eyes were large black holes. It tilted its head like it truly was a bird. Beads of sweat dripped down my face. The room was a burning hell, and I was stuck inside it. In the thing's hand was a grim reaper-like scythe. The end of the needle-sharp scythe scratched against the wall.

"D," Evie cried. "Death surround."

"S," they chanted. "Death surrounds."

"We summoned a death metal band," Ben said. "I was hoping for Shakespeare."

I screamed and yanked my hand away from the planchette, causing the Ouija board to go flying across the room.

"Are we starting the band?" Marcus joked. "You practising your screaming?" Whatever he saw in my face caused him to stand up. "Are you okay, Lacey?"

I pointed to the corner, but the thing had left.

Still laughing, Evie pushed her back against the wall.

Jess reached for me. I didn't want her hands on my body. It was she who had brought that evil thing. No, I didn't want to be anywhere near her at all. I ran from the room, almost tripping over one of the boots that Jess had taken off and carelessly thrown on the floor.

Footsteps followed me. There was a man wearing a hippy green jumper sitting on the stairs, smoking a cigarette. I brushed past him, kicking him in the elbow. I could hear cursing as I ran out into the night, slamming the door closed. A minute later, Jess was there, holding onto the crook of my arm.

"Lacey," she said. "What happened?"

"What happened?" I asked incredulously. "You know what bloody happened. You were the one to summon that thing."

"What thing?" Jess asked. "What are you talking about?"

It was the first chilly night of September. Cold enough that our breath stayed between us.

"You know what I'm talking about, Jess. I know you do. I saw the way that you were looking at me."

"You took something, didn't you?" Jess asked. "Your eyes are just as fucked as Evie's. And you're shaking."

I was shaking, no denying that. I would have to be shaking for my heart was screaming. "Get your hands off of me." I gritted my teeth, and they clanked against each other.

Jess released my arm. She peeled her coat off and handed it to me. "Take it," she said. "You're in shock or something. That pill must've—"

She was wearing a T-shirt underneath the leather coat.

It was purple, of course; it would have to be. The witches, complete with pointed hats in the middle of the T-shirt, were yellow, as was the writing above them. "Three witches," I whispered.

"What?" Jess asked. "Why do you look so disgusted? You're not a fan of their music or something? I didn't even think you knew them."

"It's you," I said. Madam Lee's warning had been about Jess; what could be wrong with a centuries-old play? The real evil had been in front of me all along. "You're evil," I said. "Your mother was right to abandon you." Jess looked as though I had slapped her. She was good at playing the victim. I'd always believed it was the big bad world out to get poor Jess. "I can see right through you," I said. My voice was shaking, matching my body. I ran then, needing to put as much distance between the two of us. I could hear the music escape as Jess opened the door and went back into the house.

I was no runner, and riding my bike was the only form of exercise that I did. When I reached Kevin's Street, I was exhausted. All I wanted was to be at home. Twice, I stopped running, and twice, I thought I heard footsteps coming behind me. My lungs hurt as I breathed. If I hadn't been so tired and scared, there's no way I would've even contemplated cutting through Red Lane but going through it would have made my journey ten minutes shorter. If I continued straight, I would get to my parents' house in fifteen; using the Red Lane route, I'd be there in five. It was a no-brainer.

I turned left and passed through a housing estate with sleepy lights faintly visible through closed curtains and blinds. My runners were light, but they made heavy sounds against the footpath—no wonder it was so quiet. There was a row of shops across from the estate. A Centra, a bookie's, a hairdresser's, and a restaurant. All of them were closed for the night. Red Lane was at the corner of the row, bordered on the other side by a long row of terraced houses. I crossed the road and walked to the mouth of the lane. It was dark. Its lips were graffitied symbols. During the day, I had no trouble passing through here. You might get the odd teenager smoking a joint, but that was about it. I had never walked through it at night. Laneways were haunted places at night, weren't they? I was about to turn and go the long way around when I heard the footsteps coming again.

I ran in and out of the light that was offered sporadically from the back of the houses. Many of them didn't have their lights on, making most of the laneway dark and full of shadows. My breathing was loud, achingly so. I couldn't hear if the footsteps were still chasing. I stopped and held my breath. The night was silent. That didn't mean much. Footsteps might not be following me, but there could be someone hiding in a dark place. My phone was still in my coat pocket. I took it out, put on the torch, and used it to light my way. I had passed the neat row of shops. To my left now was a trailing wall; beyond the wall was an industrial estate. The houses were still to my right, and the backyard walls were climbing higher and higher, mirroring the industrial estate.

Just before each towering wall, there was a little patch of grass. It wasn't wide, maybe a foot at best. During spring, these patches of grass were sewn with wildflower seeds; come summer, they would bloom in a kaleidoscope of colours. Some of the wildflowers were still blooming. I could see them under the light of my torch. One patch of them had been set alight. Here on the burnt wildflowers, I saw what I had been fearing. I shone my torch onto it.

The mask was gone. Where there should have been a face

was a red dripping smudge that looked and smelled like melting plastic. Then, there was only a blur before me. What little food was in my stomach attempted to crawl up my throat. I tried to scream, but like in a nightmare, it wouldn't leave my throat. At first, my legs wouldn't work, and I could only stare before finally I unfroze and bolted. I'll tell you, if you saw me, you would think it was a race I had been training for all my life.

When I got home, the house was quiet. I could hear my parents snoring away upstairs. I engaged all the locks on the front door and went into the kitchen. My hands were shaking so badly that it took me several attempts to turn on the tap, but I got it in the end. I could see my reflection in the mirror. My pupils weren't quite as demonic-looking as Evie's, but they weren't that far off either. Eyeliner snaked down my face. I cleaned it off with water and a paper towel and scrubbed my hands clean with the honey and milk soap Mam always kept in the kitchen.

On the worktop, my phone vibrated. It was Jess. **Did you get home okay?**

I didn't reply. What I did was something I should've done ages ago. I blocked her number. There would be no more chances for Jess. No sticking up for her when people called her weird or strange. I knew now that Madam Lee's warning had been about Jess, and I wanted nothing further to do with her.

September 25th

By Sunday night, I had gotten over my shock. Maybe Jess had summoned some entity with her Ouija board, or perhaps it had something to do with the pill I had taken. Either way, nothing had appeared to me since. When my fear subsided, all that was left was embarrassment for running away like I had. So much that I hadn't turned my phone on all weekend. I hadn't got the head for whoever would want to talk to me about my freakout at the party. I wouldn't be telling them the truth, that was for sure.

First thing on a Monday morning, we were in the studio at the other part of C.T.U.'s campus. Over here, the building was old. Over a hundred years, I'd say, but it was better kept than the Arts Building. I pulled open the glass door. Heat piped out of its ancient radiators, and the place smelled of new warmth. This type of warmth can only happen in a building that has only recently been heated after a cold spell. The terracotta tiles on the floor were beautiful. I hated their beauty. This beautiful building with its high roof used to be a Magdalene Laundry. For years these tiles, ones now quickly glossed over with a mop, were scrubbed by the women kept prisoner here. The whole place contained their memory. It was impossible not to think of them every time I entered its doors.

I turned right and walked up the sloped floor that led to the studio. I could hear the wailing before I even walked in. Evie ran to me, eyes back to normal now and hair only less messy than the last time I had seen her. Her arms wrapped around me and squeezed.

"We've been trying to contact you." Before I could ask who 'we' was, Marcus joined the two of us. He wasn't crying now, but you could tell that he had been recently.

"Why, what happened?" I asked.

"You haven't heard then?" Marcus asked.

"Heard what?" I couldn't imagine what could be so terrible that had the two of them bawling.

"Natalie's dead."

There were ten of us majoring in Theatre Studies. Natalie had never missed a day. Her face and that long swishy hair was always there. I glanced around the room. At least one of us was always out bar on exam day. Everyone was here today except Natalie. "She can't be dead." Very few people that I knew had died, and none of them were in their twenties.

"She is," Evie said. In typical Evie style, she let the tears flow down her face without any attempt at brushing them away.

"What happened to her?" I asked. That monster that I had seen flashed into my mind, and my whole body felt as though it had been pricked with needles.

"She choked on her vomit." Gary joined the three of us. He wasn't smiling for once. "Her roommate found her. What's your one's name?"

"Lisa," I said. I had never spoken with Lisa before, but I had seen her around with Natalie and heard Natalie mention her name enough times for the name to stick.

"I tried to phone you," Evie said. "I must've rung you a million times." My phone was in my backpack, but I still hadn't turned it on.

Our lecturer, a short blonde woman, walked into the

room. "Has everyone heard?" she asked—a murmur of agreement. We didn't have a class that morning. Instead, we sat in a circle and attempted to process Natalie's death.

Later, we all walked to the cafeteria, slow and solemn, as if we were behind a coffin. Sitting at a table with my classmates, I could hear Daniel, a dark-haired man with neat glasses, ask Kim, blonde and permanently lip-glossed if she thought Natalie's death had anything to do with the Macbeth curse. The two of them had been cast in the play, Daniel as Macbeth and Kim as a Weird Sister.

I had been drinking a cup of coffee and trying to comprehend Natalie's death when my head peeped up. "What's the Macbeth curse?"

"People in the play seem to get jinxed," Kim said. "I don't think there's any truth to it. It's just a bunch of superstition." Kim sipped on her flask of water, leaving a sticky coating of pink on the top. "I wonder what will happen with the play now without Lady Macbeth." She lowered her voice. "I know it sounds awful, but I hope it will continue. I was really looking forward to being in it."

Kim wasn't the only person that I heard talking about if Macbeth would go ahead. Later, back in the Arts Building, I heard more whispers, this time between Evie and Marcus.

"Ben was so looking forward to directing it, wasn't he?" Evie whispered. "I wonder, will he find a replacement for poor Natalie."

Gary wasn't meant to be part of their conversation, but he was listening in behind them. "It's hardly like he will still use Natalie for the performance, right? She wasn't going to play Hamlet's father.

Evie rolled her eyes, but neither she nor Marcus responded to Gary. Outside the window, a whoosh of crisp leaves flew past. Autumn was truly here with the death of both summer and Natalie. Jess had brought it with her board. Madam Lee was right with her warning.

October 2nd

Natalie was buried on the 2nd of October on a sunny but crisp day. All of us Theatre Studies students showed up in our black and threw red roses on top of the coffin after it was lowered into the earth. They were her favourite flowers apparently—it didn't surprise me in the least. They were beautiful too and had the cruelness of their thorns. I couldn't say I was sad about Natalie's death— we had never been friends, and it was obvious she didn't like me, but I was shocked.

Standing in the graveyard, all I could think about was what had been spelt out on the Ouija board. *Death Surrounds.* It was strange how Natalie was dead shortly after the message had come through. Even Evie was freaking out when she realised the connection. She hadn't seen what I had seen. I figured that much out after some gentle probing. I still didn't know if I truly had seen something. Whether or not I had, it hadn't reappeared since.

Jess, the absolute cheek of her, went to the funeral, not in black either, but wearing a bright red coat. Of course, only Jess would be so brazen. She looked a horror, though. Even worse than the last time. She came over to me while I was leaving the graveyard. "Lacey," she called. I looked at her, not daring to speak before I had composed myself. "I've been trying to contact you."

"You're a murderer," I spat. "You should be in there begging her family to forgive you."

"I didn't kill her." Jess fell back as though I had punched her. "It had nothing to do with me."

"You brought your fucking board to that party. You're the one that caused her death. You're poison, and I want nothing to do with you." My hands were shaking with the rage I was in.

Jess's eyes were bleeding fake tears. "I didn't—"

Whatever she said next, I didn't hear. I walked away and went into the pub where everyone was eating sandwiches, drinking soup, and talking about what a shame it all was. I sat next to Ben. He also wore black, but his shirt was red. That was okay, and it was nothing like Jess, who hadn't an ounce of black on her—nothing visible anyway.

"You gave us a shock that night," Ben said. He was the first to mention my running away.

Everyone's minds were too full of Natalie to think of me. I was the same. That run through Red Lane hardly even seemed real now. Never mind what I had seen there.

"It was frightening what Jess's board said."

"I was pretty scared myself, especially when I heard about Natalie. Death Surrounds." Ben had whiskey and coke before him. The ice clinked against the glass as he drank. "Pretty messed up. I won't be running towards playing with one of them again."

"I won't either," I said.

We left shortly afterwards. I went straight home. Mam was shaken by Natalie's death. Something similar happened to a school friend of hers in the 90s, and she was feeling the grief all over again. She was solemn and barely spoke a word to us. I pitied Mam for the reopening of an old wound, but I was grateful for the peace.

Dad, however, was more chatty than usual and tried to engage me in talking about my final year. I was grateful he was trying, but I didn't feel so much like talking.

"What about that play, the one poor Natalie was meant to be in?" Everyone called her poor Natalie now. She would've hated that.

"I don't know," I said.

"You wanted to audition for it, didn't you? I saw you carrying the play around with you. Why didn't you audition in the end?"

"Nerves," I said. Not a lie. Only I was afraid of the wrong thing.

"Would you go for Natalie's part now? It would be a way of honouring her." Dad opened the biscuit tin and took out a custard cream. He held the packet towards me, and I took one. I needed the sugar.

"It wouldn't seem right," I said. I scoffed the first biscuit down and went onto my second. The only thing was that it wasn't Natalie's part. It was meant to be mine. It was a pity I hadn't realised that Madam Lee was warning me about Jess, and I wouldn't be in this situation. If I had known, maybe poor Natalie might still be alive.

October 9th

Two days after Natalie's funeral, Ben rang, asking if I'd consider being his Lady Macbeth. "You were always the one I wanted to play her."

"I can't," I said. "It wouldn't be right. Not to poor Natalie." There, I was also saying it. It's not brilliant any more, but poor Natalie.

"I'll just have to ask again tomorrow and tomorrow—"

"Goodbye, Ben," I said.

True to Ben's word, he kept calling back, and I kept saying no. "How about we meet for coffee, and I'll try and convince you in person?"

I agreed.

"Tomorrow then, on the ninth," Ben said. "Nine is my

lucky number, so hopefully, you'll agree then."

We arranged to meet under the arch at Enda's Park at 5 p.m. I arrived five minutes early, but Ben was already there, waiting. He smiled when he saw me. He looked good in his jeans and blazer, but Ben always looked good.

"There she is," Ben said. "I was worried you wouldn't turn up."

"Never mind not showing up; I'm early," I said.

"Eager to discuss the play," he said.

"Theatre is my life."

We walked to the little coffee shop next to the arch. A few people sat inside. They must've just left work because they were all smartly dressed.

We ordered coffee and sat down. I felt like one of those businesspeople discussing a huge deal before Ben smiled. He had little wrinkles around his eyes that most people my age didn't.

"How old are you, Ben?" I asked abruptly.

"Twenty-seven," he said. "Want to know my date of birth?"

"You're okay." I tilted my head, inspecting Ben. I knew he had directed several plays in Dublin and acted in a few.

But I had no idea what he did here. "What do you do all day?"

"Well, at the moment, I'm writing my own play. That's cutting into most of my time. If I do a decent enough job at directing Macbeth, there's the chance that my uncle will let me produce that in Draoícht."

"What's your uncle got to do with Draoicht?"

"He owns it," Ben said. "He didn't want me near it. He said it wouldn't look good because we're related. He forgets this isn't my first rodeo. Not by a long shot. Still, if Macbeth goes well and he lets me produce my play, it would be doing me a favour."

"People were wondering if you'd still go ahead with Macbeth without Natalie in it."

"Even if I wanted to change the play, I would have no choice. He said he would let me direct Macbeth or nothing at all. It's the only test he'll assign to me."

"Either way, you're going to need a Lady Macbeth," I said.

"You were always my first choice."

"Why're you so eager for me to play her?"

The waitress, a young woman with blue hair and wide blue eyes, brought drinks over to the table.

Mine was a cinnamon and apple latte. I drank it. It was good and comforting. Although, I should've ordered decaf with the way my nerves were going. Sitting here with Ben, I was okay, but at home, my mind would wander, and I would think about what I had seen on the night Natalie died.

"I've seen you act before," Ben said. "I know you're more than capable. Also, don't get me wrong: you are my Lady Macbeth. You're my vision of what she should be."

"What have you seen me in before?" I asked. Although I had been in a few local productions I didn't realise Ben had seen me in anything.

Ben listed three of the plays that I had been in since first year. "Gary dragged me along with him." Ben added a sachet of sugar to his double espresso and sipped it. "When I saw you up there, I know this sounds mad, but I said one day I'll get her to act in something that I'm directing. Then I saw you that night of the fireworks, and I was delighted. I didn't want to tell you I knew who you were."

"But you're telling me now," I said.

"I'm pouring out my heart, hoping you'll listen and say yes."

"Alright then," I said. I was still thinking of poor

Natalie, but it would be cruel of me to reject Ben's offer now. Especially when I knew how much it meant to him. "I'll be your Lady Macbeth."

"Well then, Lacey, you've just made me a very happy man."

October 17th

It was only October now. I know that sounds strange when we were past the halfway point, but we were so in the thick of it that it was overwhelming. Every café I passed had a pumpkin spiced this and that advertised in their windows. And every shopfront was decorated with skeletons and witches. Speaking of witches, I hadn't spoken with that one since Natalie's funeral. There were a few times that I thought I saw her around campus, but on closer inspection, it would never actually be her.

Jess would love all these horrors in the shopfront. They were her kin. Only last year we had strolled through these streets together. Now, I hated the decorations. I had no choice but to pass them walking to the theatre. I kept my eyes straight ahead, but I knew what surrounded me. In two more weeks, all of the Halloween decorations would be gone, and Christmas displays would take their place. That was a soothing thought. Passing by Supermacs, an arm wrapped around my own. I knew it was Evie by the sweet perfume she was wearing.

"Hello, Lady Macbeth," she said.

Evie was beyond ecstatic when she found out that I was going to be in the play. "Hello, Weird Sister," I said. I'd never call her a witch. No way. Not a hope.

"Are you excited?" she asked.

"For the play?" I asked.

"Yes, for the Scottish Play, life, and the joy of being alive." I peeked at her eyes, and the pupils were normal size. Just regular Evie then.

"I am excited," I said. We had already done three readthroughs of the play, and each one went well. It turns out it wasn't that big of a deal that I was replacing Natalie when she had only been Lady Macbeth for two read-throughs. She was only warming my seat for me.

Evie and myself continued our walk arm and arm to Draíocht. This was my favourite part of rehearsals. The readthroughs were always full of fun and possibilities before it got too real and the big stress began. I was enjoying every bit of it now.

"You ever see Jess anymore?" Evie asked.

"No," I said.

"Am I allowed to ask why?"

"She wasn't who I thought she was," I said. "And that incident with the Ouija board."

"I thought that was why; I just wanted to be sure." Evie smiled at me. She had a little pink diamond on her tooth today.

We continued walking towards Draíocht. It was just at the beginning of Catherine's Street— a bustling long street with various shops, including a vintage store, a tattoo parlour, and two record stores. You'd never know Draíocht was situated down the narrow alleyway only for the sign above the alley. The cobblestone alley opened up to a large courtyard that had two marble seats in front of a large Georgian building with ivy-covered walls. The arch-shaped double doors were closed. Evie pushed one, and we entered the theatre. The ceilings were high and white, like the walls, and the floors were wooden. At the back of the foyer was a large, curved stairwell that led to the dress circle and the gods.

Ben stood next to the box office desk, talking to the receptionist. My heart did a little flip. Sure, it was obvious that my body fancied him, but my mind was catching up with the idea now too. I was doing my best to distract my thoughts, but it was getting harder and harder to do.

"Hello ladies," he said. "Another beautiful day out there, isn't it?"

"Just splendid," Evie said.

I don't think I would ever enjoy autumn again. It was a shame because I used to love it. "It's nice and bright," I said. It wouldn't be for long though. Not with the way that the nights were drawing in.

Evie and myself walked into the auditorium. Our circle of chairs had been unmoved from the stage since yesterday. Kim, my blonde classmate with the lip gloss addiction, was already there. Daniel was sitting beside her, staring at the play in his hands. We might have been married in the play, but in real life, we rarely spoke, and he was about as interesting as one of the battered leaves on the ground. On Daniel's other side was Dervla, a second-year Theatre Studies student who was playing a Weird Sister. Dervla had silky blonde hair and an upturned nose so she could sniff out the gossip she so loved. Next to Dervla was Gary, who was playing Macduff. The only other actor I knew was Marcus, who was playing Banquo. Everyone else was new to me.

"Hello, hello." Stuart, the actor playing King Duncan, strolled into the room. He was somewhere in his thirties and already sported fully silver hair on his head and beard. "Town is blazing with Halloween. Everyone excited for it?"

"I can't stand Halloween," I said. "Macbeth is more than enough spook for me."

Evie's hand was on her mouth." Oh Lacey, you didn't," she said.

"I did." I wasn't ashamed of it either. "Halloween is not my favourite time of the year. Christmas is more my vibe. Imagine, not long after Christmas, Macbeth will be on the stage."

"This is blasphemy to the Theatre Gods," Stuart stood up. His hand on his heart.

I couldn't tell if he was joking or not. "What, are the Theatre Gods obsessed with Halloween?" I asked.

"You don't know," Evie said.

"So they are obsessed with it," I said.

Evie pointed to the title of the play. "You can't say this

word in a Theatre. Haven't you not wondered why we keep calling it the Scottish Play?"

"Don't you know about the curse?" What have they been teaching you in that college of yours?" Stuart asked.

At that moment, Ben strolled into the room. He seemed like a different man than what I had met at the bus stop; he was more confident and taller. "Everyone should be here in the next five minutes, and we'll get started. How does that sound?" Seeing the look on my face, he added, "Lacey, are you okay?"

"She said the cursed word," Evie said. "She didn't know."

Usually, something like this wouldn't have bothered me as much, but Stuart and Evie seemed genuinely frightened. And I was still a nervous wreck after what had happened with Jess and then poor Natalie.

"It's okay," Ben said. He was smiling, but I could see the fear on his face. "Just reverse the curse."

"How do I reverse the curse?" Everyone was staring; I could feel their eyes on me. Stuart was both scared and annoyed, while Evie was terrified.

"Leave the theatre. Spin around three times and spit over your left shoulder," Evie said. "And either curse or recite a line of Shakespeare. I'd recommend the Shakespeare since you're already cursed."

"I'm not cursed," I said. "Don't you dare say that."

"Right now, you are." Stuart curled his lip at me. "You can try and reverse it all you want, but I bet that you've cursed the production now. That's how it always goes," he tutted and rolled his eyes.

"Lads," Ben said. "The production isn't cursed. All Lacey has to do is reverse the curse, and we can forget all about it."

My hands were shaking. I rubbed them on my black turtleneck. "Exit the stage, spin around three times, and spit over my left shoulder?" My voice was also shaking.

"And your line of Shakespeare," Evie said. She was smiling, but I knew I had hurt her with my outburst. "The go-to line is 'angels and ministers of grace defend us.'"

I nodded and reversed my steps until I was outside. I spun around three times—anti-clockwise. A tip I remembered from Jess—if you want to bring something into your life, then spin clockwise, and to get rid of something, then it's anticlockwise. I most certainly wanted to get rid of something. I spat. I said *"angels and ministers of grace defend us"* repeatedly in my head as I walked out of the door. But that wasn't the line that came from my mouth. What came out instead was: "From the pricking of my thumbs, something wicked this way comes."

Overhead high on the roof, the birds cawed along with me, and a whoosh of leaves swept past, taking away the curse—I hoped.

"Either you're learning the wrong lines, you've said the cursed word, or you're having a breakdown. Which one is it?" Margaret, who was playing Hecate, stood next to me. I hadn't heard her approach; such was the loudness of my fear.

"I said the cursed word," I said. "I didn't even know you weren't meant to say it."

"Well, you've rid yourself of the curse now, so don't worry." She had the softest and puffiest hair that I had ever seen. It was like a cloud, only red. I often had to stop myself from patting her on the head.

She linked my arm, and we strolled back inside. "The production is curse-free," Margaret said.

There was a little clap all around. Although I smiled, I didn't dare believe it, for there were bats doing laps inside my stomach.

October 25th

Rehearsals were going well. Out of all the cast, Stuart was the only one that I didn't bond with. It was a shame that Lady Macbeth chickened out from killing King Duncan because I would've loved to slide a sword into him. Only while acting, of course.

Evie and myself often walked to Draíocht together, passing all those little monsters. She knew they repulsed me and would do her best to distract me from the creepy window displays.

"I have a feeling about what the answer will be, but I'll ask anyway: Are you coming to the Halloween party?" Evie asked.

The Macbeth cast were all going out together on

Halloween night to The Roaring Lion—one of the best pubs in Castlebridge. Everyone was going to dress up. "I'm not going to go," I said. I patted Evie on the shoulder. She was like a little puppy and lapped up any form of attention, especially touch. "You have a great time, though."

"It won't be the same without you, but I can't kidnap you," she sighed. "I'll just have to pretend that you're there."

"I'm not that fun anyway," I said. "I would just be learning my lines and going on about assignments." This was true about me now. During my first and second years of college, I was mad for all the parties and always did my assignments at the last minute. How the wild times had fallen.

"You are fun," Evie was already linking me. I swear she was afraid of getting lost, but her grip tightened. So, when she began skipping, I had no choice but to skip along with her. I tell you, for a pint-sized woman, she had some strength.

Half an hour later, I was standing next to Ben, watching Evie. We were now rehearsing from the stage, mostly with our copies of the play in hand, but it was good to be up there. This play, the Scottish Play, was the first one that I had ever been part of in Draíocht, and it was always wonderful to take to the stage in a new venue, even if we were still early into rehearsals.

"How are you doing today, Lacey?" Ben asked. "Well, over your shock at cursing yourself?" He smiled at me in that way of his.

"I am, thank you," I said. I kept my eyes focused on Evie. She was standing in the middle with Kim and Dervla on either side of her. Mad to see her next to someone without linking them. I was fine at first. I had heard them say their lines repeatedly, but seeing them on stage was different. I had done research into the curse of the Scottish Play, and there were claims that Shakespeare had used real witches' incantations and they had cursed the play for revenge.

"You okay?" Ben asked. He had his hand on my arm, and his eyes were on mine. I didn't enjoy crushes. They could make you think and act like a fool. "I'm fine. I'm just going to get a drink of water." I was away before I could do anything stupid. I grabbed my flask from my backpack and went out to the foyer. It was true I was thirsty and did need to fill it before I was needed. I descended the stairs to the basement and went into the staff kitchen. Margaret, queen of the witches herself, had just made a cup of tea, and her cauldron-shaped mug was blowing steam.

"What do you think of my new mug?" she asked me. "I thought it would help me get into character. I know Hecate only has a few lines, but I wanted to do them justice."

"I don't like all the witchy stuff. It gives me the creeps. Did you know that they were the ones who put a curse on the play?"

Margaret laughed. "You know the backstory of the play? About King James and his fear of witches?"

I knew a little about it. But history had never been my thing. I told Margaret as much.

"King James got it into his head that witches were out to get him. He wrote a whole book about witches that led to hundreds of innocent women being murdered. When Will wrote the play, James was sitting on his witch-hating throne, and Will added the witches to please him.
If there's any curse on the Scottish Play, it's rooted in fear and has nothing to do with witchcraft. Not that there's anything wrong with witches."

"I'm not so sure about that," I said.

"About the curse or the witches?" Margaret asked. She drank from her cauldron with the steam framing her face like a fog. Whatever she was drinking must've been scalding.

I didn't want her to give me a big speech about witchcraft again, so I told her I believed the play was cursed.

"Could it be your belief in the curse that makes it cursed? Belief is a powerful thing."

She was starting to sound a bit like Jess now. I didn't like that. "Could be," I shrugged. I filled my flask, and we went back upstairs. The witches were just leaving the stage. A wink from Ben and that distracted me from thinking about the curse, not Margaret and her good intentions. The rest of the day went by well. When it was time to go home, it was October dark outside. Even here in the centre of the town, I could see the star-riddled sky. Evie was admiring it as I wished her a good night.

"The sky is a wonder tonight, isn't it?" Evie asked.

"It's nice enough," I concurred. "A little too cold for me, though." I was only wearing a light denim jacket over my T-shirt, but I'd be fine once I started moving.

"Goodbye, girls." Margaret came out of the door behind us and wrapped her arms around herself. "There is a chill in it," she said. "But at least it's not raining anymore."

My bike was attached to the railing at the side of the building. I unlocked it. Evie was only living five minutes away in a little bedsit. I could see her walking towards it as I cycled out onto the road. There weren't many cars around because it was after ten o'clock at night. The lights coming from these few cars seemed exceptionally bright. I ignored the lights as best as I could and cycled faster and was just getting into a nice flow when it happened. True, the night was cold, but I hadn't reckoned there being ice on the road. The front wheel shuddered, and the handlebars vibrated. Instead of just gliding on the ice, in my panic, I squeezed the break. Slow motion falling. Images flashed through my head: Jess and her final departure from my life, me in my naiveté saying Macbeth in the theatre and the fear as I watched the Weird Sisters on the stage. On the ground now. A whoosh of colour in my eyes: red. It would have to be the colour of pain. It was everywhere. My body throbbed.

A car sped past me. It was just as well that I was in the cycle lane. The next car didn't drive past. I saw its hazard lights, and then it pulled in behind me. The car was green, but I wouldn't have been able to tell that in the dark. I only knew because I had seen the car before. Ben got out.

"Lacey," he said. He rushed over to me. "Are you okay?"

"I don't know," I said. I didn't. My legs burnt—my right one in particular."

"Do you think you can walk?" he asked.

That was answered a moment later when Ben helped me to my feet. I wrapped my arm around his neck, and he helped me get to the car. Ben retrieved my bike and put it in the boot.

Sitting, I saw the rip down the side of my jeans and the blood oozing from the scratches on the exposed skin.

"You alright?" he asked.

"I'll live," I said, dropping my head against the headrest. "Lucky for me, you were there."

The accident had put me in a daze; I didn't know we were going to the hospital until we pulled up outside of the A & E. We walked to the reception. There was no queue, which was something.

The fluorescents in the waiting room stung my eyes. There was also a strong smell of a chemical cleaner. These two factors caused my eyes to water.

Ben thought I was crying at first. "Do you need painkillers? I could ask them to get you something?"

"It's the lights," I said. "And the bleach. It always kills my eyes. My mother says I'm sensitive to just about everything."

There was a TV above the snack machine playing an episode of Judge Judy. Ben and myself stared at it vacantly.

"Do you think I cursed myself?"

"Cursed yourself?" Ben asked. He looked bemused. "Why would you think you cursed yourself?"

"When I called it Macbeth instead of the Scottish play. That was only a week ago, and now I'm after falling off my bike."

"You fell from your bike because the roads were icy. Nothing to do with a curse." There was tension on my face, and he saw it. "Honestly, don't worry. Anyone would've fallen."

"I never told you why I didn't want to audition in the first place," I said slowly. I didn't know how much to reveal. The belief in a curse was one thing, but agreeing with a psychic was something else. I rubbed my hands together, feeling the skin which had become winter rough. "I went to see a psychic, and she told me to stay away from three witches." I told him all about Madam Lee and then seeing Jess's t-shirt. Ben let me talk and didn't say a word until he knew I was finished speaking.

"That's very strange," he said. "Very strange, especially with your one wearing that T-shirt on the night Natalie died. But strange things happen the whole time. All I can say is I'm glad you're not friends with her—she was a real weird one."

"So, you don't think the warning was real?"

"Not a hope," Ben said. "Yeah, it's a bit of a coincidence, but you could link three witches to anything if you want to. Don't be worrying. And if there's truth to it, then it's about Jess."

I knew the warning was real. I didn't need to convince Ben, but hearing him say it was about Jess was all the reassurance I needed. Of course, it was about Jess. I shouldn't even be doubting it. Being in the play had inadvertently led me to fall off my bike. Sure, that might have happened anyway. "Okay," I said. I settled into the chair. Despite the pain in my body, I was comfortable sitting there with Ben beside me.

"I proclaim you curse free." He waved his hand like a wand. "Don't be worrying about wicked witches or curses anymore."

I laughed. One that came from deep within my stomach,

and the knot that had been there for the last week unravelled.

Ben stayed with me in the hospital. I kept telling him to leave, and I'd get a taxi home, but he wouldn't listen. As far as A & E visits go, we didn't have to stay there for too long. At 1 a.m., we walked back to the car. My body, my legs in particular, were badly scratched and bruised, but I was okay. I was lucky. But I had been warned, both by the hospital staff and Ben that I shouldn't be going anywhere on my bike without a helmet strapped to my head.

Ben and myself bought two takeaway coffees from the vending machine before leaving, but the heat from the Styrofoam cups did little to keep out the chill of the night.

"It's going to be a bad winter," Ben said. "A very bad one."

"Snow would be nice," I said. I know it's like that song, but I've dreamt of a white Christmas ever since I was a child. I think only once in my life did I get to experience one.

Inside the car, it was as cold as it was outside. We drove out of the parking lot, passing a heavily pregnant woman and her companion. We didn't see anyone else on the drive through town. Not a sinner nor a saint around.

"Have you decided if you're going to the Halloween party with us?" Ben asked. His eyes were on the road, but he glanced at me for a second. "It would be great if you could make it. It'll be a laugh."

"I'm not a fan of Halloween," I said.

"But you're a fan of parties," Ben said. "And a fan of me?"

Well, what could I say? He was right on both parts. "Do I need to have a costume?"

"I don't think it's a requirement," he said. He pulled in a few houses away from my parents' house. "But I can hardly believe that I've found an actor who doesn't enjoy dressing up."

I did love costumes. "I'll go. Only I've no idea what I'll wear. What are you dressing up as?"

"That's a surprise," he said.

I had my hand on the door. "I better get moving. Early start in the morning. Thanks for looking after me."

"You're welcome."

There was a heavy pause. It probably only lasted a few seconds, but it seemed longer. We said goodbye, and I left the car. Only as I saw his headlights drive away did I remember that my bike was in his car.

October 31st

The rest of the week went by smoothly. There were only two days of college left until we got our Halloween break. I could've stayed home and rested, but I'd only be coddled by my mother, who enjoyed treating me like a baby. Rehearsals were going well too. Ben was morphing into his directorial role and getting more focused every time we rehearsed. He'd a good temper on him too. Some directors could become right terrors, but to be fair, that usually only happened when we approached opening night. I don't think Ben will become like that. There's a sweetness to him. On that first night after the accident, he drove me home after rehearsals. Leaving me and my scraped but otherwise unharmed bike outside of the house. Each night since he's been bringing me home. I've told him there's no need when I only live a fifteen-minute walk away, but he's been insistent. It's been nice having that extra time with him. Two nights ago, he came in for a cup of tea. The parents even stayed out of the way, with Mam only peeping her head in to say hello before she disappeared.

On the day of Halloween, I found myself looking forward to the party. I split the day between doing my college assignments and reading my lines. Mam did scold me on this, saying I was getting obsessive about rehearsing. I told her obsession was required for excellence.

"And Lacey," Mam had said, "what good are you going to be to anyone if you fall down dead from stressing yourself out? Already one Lady Macbeth has died; we don't want there to be two."

I'm sorry to say this, but I had just forgotten about poor Natalie until Mam noted this. Imagine if she had lived; my life would be going in a completely different direction. My assignments would be done anyway. There'd be no stressing over them. I probably wouldn't be doing anything for Halloween tonight. I'd hide myself away and watch something light on Netflix. But Natalie was dead. Her death gave me my role—it wasn't in vain.

Mam knocked on my bedroom door. She knew I was going out tonight. She didn't seem to mind me having fun now that Jess was out of the way.

"You look lovely," she said.

I did look nice. I inspected my costume in the mirror. I was a mermaid. I know not scary, but I had enough darkness in my life to last forever. It was a simple costume: just a bikini top with a fishtail skirt. I had painted scales onto my skin and put on a blue wig. My eye shadow was a mixture of blue and green, and my lips were painted coral.

"Only you would be better putting on a T-shirt over that bikini top," Mam said. "You'll freeze your skin off, and everyone will think you're meant to be a snake."

I'll give it to her; she was cute with her newest insult. I could take that one. "Tell you what, I'll bring a coat, and then there'll be no need to worry."

Mam gave up the battle. I put on my warmest coat and waited outside for Ben. He wasn't drinking that night. He said there was no way he would attempt to get a taxi on a Halloween night. And walking, forget about it. It wasn't ghouls or goblins he was afraid of but teenagers with eggs. I thought that last bit was funny. "What's so scary about eggs? They're great for your hair, you know," I said to him.

"I have got a fear of them. What can I say," Ben said.

It suited me just fine. I wasn't planning on having a wild night anyway. I hadn't had much in the way of drink since the night that Natalie died.

Ben arrived right on time. "I love the face," he said. "Are you a fish or something?"

"A mermaid," I said. "But you got close enough. And you're what, Dracula?"

His hair was combed back, and he had plastic fangs in his mouth with two lines of fake blood running down his chin. "Just a standard vampire. I couldn't wish for as lofty a title as Dracula. But I'm honoured that you would think I was him."

Most, if not all, of the trick-or-treaters had gone home by the time we drove through town, but there were plenty of teenagers wearing masks. In town, it was mayhem. I hadn't thought it would be this busy, especially with Halloween falling on a weeknight.

Ben parked his car on a side street, and we walked to The Roaring Lion. Jess and myself used to go there a lot during the first year of college, but we didn't go as much in second year. I only hoped she wouldn't be there tonight.

If she were, I'd just have to ignore the witch.

"There's meant to be a great band playing here tonight," Ben said as we walked into the venue.

"What?" I asked, my voice loud. "What did you say?"

"The band," Ben pointed at the stage.

The band were dressed in old-school monster costumes. There was Frankenstein as lead singer, Frankenstein's bride on guitar, a mummy on bass, and a werewolf on drums. The song that had been playing ended, and "Season of the Witch" began.

I scanned the area. Just about everyone there was in costumes, so it would've been difficult to recognise the cast. "See anyone?" I asked.

Ben shook his head. The place was packed. "We'll look around," he said into my ear. We walked deeper into the venue and climbed up a short flight of stairs that led to the next level. Here, it wasn't as busy, but it was still packed enough that we had to push our way through the crowds.

We found the cast sitting on plush purple couches with a table overladen with drinks between them. Evie ran over and squeezed us both in turn. "Come sit with me." No guessing who Evie was in her green dress and ivy wrapped around her body. She had even dyed her hair bright red to match Uma Thurman's Poison Ivy. She grabbed my hand and led me next to her. Ben joined on my other side. He was only there for a few seconds before being ambushed by Stuart and drawn into a debate about God only knows what. I took off my coat, feeling suddenly very naked, sitting there in my bikini top. Maybe this happened at the ripe old age of 22.

Evie was drinking a green cocktail with what looked like an eyeball on a cocktail stick in the glass. She handed me a matching drink. "I bought it for you," she said. "I was manifesting your arrival for the last ten minutes."

Sometimes, she reminded me of Jess. I didn't like that she did, but they were different. There was nothing evil about Evie. "Thank you." I took the drink from her. It was definitely an eyeball on the stick—candied but still an eyeball. "What is it?"

"Zombies eyeballs," she said. "The sweets are vegan if you're worried. And they're soaked in rum," she said into my ear. "They taste delicious too."

They tasted delicious, as did the cocktail. Enough that within the hour, I had spent €50 on them and was well on my way to being scuttered. After drinking my fourth cocktail, Evie dragged me onto the floor to dance to the

"Time Warp." She had shaved the sides of her hair off and cut ivy leaves into it. I only noticed it there as we were dancing. She really did go all out on her costume.

I saw it then, standing at the edge of the crowd. It wore the same black coat with the red plague doctor's mask. The scythe was in its hand. Even with the music blaring, I swear I could hear it scratching against the wall.

Evie was holding my hands and swaying from side to side. I had been animatedly dancing with her until I saw the figure standing against the wall. I froze. Evie squeezed my hands and then shook them. "You okay, Lace?" she asked.

"Over there," I said into her ear. "The one in the plague doctor's mask. Do you see it?"

Evie scanned the dance floor. "Where?"

"It was right there," I said.

"Did you like the mask?" Evie screamed into my ear. I pulled my hands from her grasp.

"Did you see it, Evie?" Already my throat hurt from straining my voice all night.

"No," Evie said. She twirled around and around.

"I need to get some water," I said.

"What?" Evie said.

I mimicked drinking. "Water," I said.

Dervla was late to our gathering and had only arrived. I could see her passing by the dancefloor with her phone in her hand. "Dervla," Evie screeched before running over and wrapping her arms around her.

I slipped away from the dance floor and went back upstairs. Here, I had a good view of the crammed ground floor. Almost every costume you could imagine was there, but no sign of the Plague Doctor existed. Maybe I hadn't seen it. It was possible. Those cocktails were strong. My head was still spinning, but I sobered right up. I slid in through the people around the bar, who seemed more content, marvelling over costumes and flirting, than rushing to get a drink.

The bartender, dressed as the Joker, handed me a pint glass of water. I was sipping it when I turned around and saw the figure—the black hollows where eyes should be stared at me. The glass slipped from my hand and shattered on the ground. I took a step forward, and the figure did the same. We were only a foot apart, and if it wanted to, it could slice me with its scythe. It struck the bottom of the weapon against the ground, and I ran to my left. In my confusion, I thought the way would lead me towards the couches and to Ben, but if I wanted that outcome, I should've turned right. When I reached the doorway that fed into a different part of the bar, I realised my mistake. I looked over my shoulder, and sure enough, it was behind me. This time, it was dragging the tip of its scythe against the floor. There was no choice, and I continued onwards. There was a narrow hallway after the doorway. It was quieter here, so people would often gather to converse. The area was even more packed than usual, with at least ten people deep in conversation. The spiders dangling from the ceiling and the thick webs on the wall made the compact space so much worse.

I pushed my way through a handful of Harley Quinns, a Barbie, and a zombie.

At the end of the hallway, I turned around and saw the Plague Doctor at the top of the entrance. There were twelve feet between me and it. It kept walking. Its steps were slow and measured, almost like a grotesque version of a bridal march. I ran once again. This time, out of the corridor and into the next area of the bar. A DJ stood on a platform, bobbing his head with his top hat sitting perilously on his head. People were grooving on the dancefloor to a remix of "Thriller."

If I kept going straight, I'd come to the smoking area. Back in first year, I used to merrily smoke away with Jess but quit when the insides of my fingers turned yellow. At the back of the smoking area, situated between the used kegs, was a door that led into an alleyway. Bands sometimes played where the DJ was currently set up and would park their vehicles in the alleyway to transport their equipment. I knew about the door, but I thought it was always locked until, out of sheer curiosity, I discovered it was open.

Grey smoke swirled. It was too busy here, like the rest of the pub. Another reason that inspired me to quit smoking: I hated the way bodies were packed out here and the poor ventilation for the dozens of cigarettes fogging up the place. Above, the tin ceiling might have protected people from the rain, but there was only a six-inch space between the wall and ceiling for the smoke to escape.

I turned around, and sure enough, the figure was behind me. Strobe lights rotated on the ceiling and bounced off the mask, illuminating the red. For a moment, I debated screaming for help, but what if it went after the crowd? No. I wouldn't take the chance. I ran straight for the poster-covered door. Its handle was loose enough that I feared it would fall off as I pushed. But with a whoosh, it opened into the dark alley. I closed the door behind me, hoping that it hadn't seen me disappear. There was a beat of calm. The threat was at the other side of the wooden wall. I was free. If I turned to the right, the road would take me anywhere. At the very worst, if it did follow me, getting help on the Main Road or running to the Garda Station, only five minutes away, would be easier—a bang on the door. I wasn't waiting around to greet my visitor. I turned right, eyes so pictured on the road that should've been there that I didn't see the new fence blocking off my escape. I ran straight into it, and a spotlight came on overhead.

I screamed. Not blood curling but blood freezing and my whole body felt as though it had been dropped into a tub of ice-cold water.

Scratching against the tarmac, I refused to turn around. Not yet. There was another door on the fence. This one had a steel handle. I turned it but I knew already that it would be locked. The fence and door were nothing like the cheap job in the smoking area. This one was meant to keep people out. There was even barbed wire at the very top of the steel fence and a camera pointing onto the road.

Scratching again, I turned around very slowly. It was

there in the darkness at the back of the alleyway where the spotlight barely reached. I could just make out its beak-like nose. I didn't want to see it anymore.

I bolted for the door and pulled the flimsy handle. It fell off in my hand. I tried pushing, but it was pointless when the door had to be pulled in my direction. I attempted to nudge my foot underneath the wood, but there was no space. I hit the door. "Help me," I screamed. "Help me."

Music blared in the smoking room.

Movement in the shadows.

Then the door pushed in on me.

"Lacey?" Ben stood there. It was the first time that I had seen his vampire makeup in the light, and I could see the clumps of white on his skin. Most of the blood had disappeared from around his chin too. "I've been looking everywhere for you. Evie too." Before I could warn him not to close the door, he did.

"It's trying to kill me," I said. My eyes darted around the area. There were six kegs and a humongous-looking motorbike. The figure wasn't there.

"It's gone," I said.

"Who's gone?" Ben asked, putting his hand on my waist. I could feel the heat emanating from his palm.

"It disappeared," I said.

"You're telling me someone scaled that wall." Ben looked from the fence to the wall that enclosed the space. Both of them were over twelve feet tall, and both had barbed wire on the top. "They would be some climber doing that, and in costume, sure, they'd be professionals."

"If it was once human, it isn't anymore," I said.

"I'm not following," Ben said.

I took a deep breath. "On the night that we did the Ouija Board." I closed my eyes. "On the night that Natalie died, I saw something in the room with us. That's why I freaked out and ran away. Then, on the way home, I saw it again."

"What did you see?" Ben asked.

"It was—" I licked my lips. "It wore a long black cloak and had one of those plague doctor's masks on. And it had one of those things that the Grim Reaper carries. The thing with the curved blade."

Ben didn't say anything for a moment. "And you thought you saw it again tonight?"

"Yes," I whispered. "It took Natalie. Now it wants me."

Ben put his hands on my waist and stared into my eyes. "I think you got a fright, Lacey. It's been a crazy few weeks. Anyone could imagine things. Tonight, you saw someone dressed like a plague doctor, and your imagination went crazy."

"No. I know what I saw."

"There are at least three people in there with plague doctor masks on. You saw one of them, and you thought it was chasing you. Then you got locked in here, and that didn't help."

"What about on that night?" I asked.

"Marcus has a huge masquerade mask in his room. Granted, it's a different type of mask, but you were flying off your head. It's no surprise your imagination went wild."

It was my turn to be silent. I ingested all that he had said and nodded. "I hope you're right."

"Well, I'm definitely not left," he said.

I laughed. And all the fear faded away.

"Can we get out of here?" he asked.

"We're trapped," I said. "The door can only open from the other side." On those words, it opened, and Evie stood in the doorway. Before the door could close behind Evie, Ben used one of the empty kegs to prop the door open.

"Lacey!" She ran towards me. Her arms wrapped around my neck, tight enough I feared I would choke. "We were so worried about you. I couldn't find you anywhere."

I wasn't sure what to say. It had felt so real, but now I wasn't sure. If the figure had been here, then Ben would've seen it. Wouldn't he? "I just got a fright," I said. "The costumes really do freak me out."

"Might be best to call it a night?" Ben asked. "I've had enough, myself."

I nodded.

The three of us went back into the smoking area. We said goodbye to Evie and the rest of the cast and walked towards his car. It was still early—not yet midnight, and people were queuing to get into the pubs. There was a 20-person line to get into The Roaring Lion.

"You feeling any better?" Ben asked.

"Much better now," I said. I was. That's the thing. Everything that had just transpired was already beginning to feel like a dream—or a nightmare. "I hope you don't think I'm nuts."

The face that Ben made was so earnest that I wanted to kiss him—alright, I had been wanting to kiss him for such a long time. "Honestly, so much has happened to you recently. It's no wonder you're experiencing trauma. And you didn't even want to go out tonight. We should've stayed at home and watched a movie." I didn't know if he meant me and him or the whole cast. Walking to the pub, we took the shorter route through a narrow street. Neither of us crossed the road to go that way; instead, we went the longer route, which was lit up by fast-food shops and a late-night Centra.

I saw Ben looking at a pizzeria. "You hungry?" I asked him.

"Not for food," he said. Before I could read into his response, he said: "Blood, I'm hungry for blood. Vampire, remember?" he pointed at his teeth that were fang-free until he slipped them out of his pocket and put them back on.

I laughed.

"You know that you saw a plague doctor, a symbol of death, makes so much sense too. It's interesting how our brains work. And there was the whole curse and psychic malarkey. No wonder you got freaked out."

When the well-lit street ended, we turned onto Merville Road. There was a posh dress shop with a pretty pastel pink interior and the same pink colours on the walls inside. I had always loved the look of the place. It was the shop where I had picked out my Debs dress years before. It was outside the shop where Ben and I stopped talking and kissed for the first time. It was a good kiss. That's all I'll say. When the kiss was over, we walked back to the car, hand in hand.

I was buzzing when I got home. The kiss almost rid my mind of what had happened in The Roaring Lion. Almost, for that night when I dreamt, it wasn't Ben that I dreamt about but the Plague Doctor.

November 21st

The first three weeks of November were some of the best of my life. Everything went so smoothly. I was the first out of the cast to have their lines down. Sure, I still needed a bit of work to perfect my delivery, but there was no tripping over my tongue trying to remember my lines. I was bang on time with all my assignments and was way ahead of my schedule.

Ben and myself were officially seeing each other, but we tried not to let the rest of the cast know. But they did anyway. Even Mam was in good form. She was excited for Christmas. I was too. I guess I had inherited that passion from her.

And the Plague Doctor? No sign of it. I wasn't sure what

had happened on Halloween. Ben might have been right, and it was a trauma-based hallucination. Or Jess had invited it into our world on the night of the Ouija board. Maybe it was easier to see it because it was Halloween. I didn't know. As long as it didn't appear again, I didn't care.

On the 21st of November, I woke up with a cold—my first one of the season. It was a rare thing for me to even get a cold. Since I started playschool, Mam always had me shielded with a good multivitamin. It was a habit that I had taken with me into adulthood. Every morning, just before eating my breakfast, I would take a dose of vitamins. The odd time I would get sick, but it wasn't often. I know a cold isn't a huge deal, but I didn't like how it made me feel disoriented and lethargic. Nevertheless, the day and the show had to go on. I took my multivitamin as usual and added a huge dose of Vitamin C to flush that cold out of my system.

It didn't have a huge impact on me in college. It was the one day when all the classes were in theory, so I could just sit there and jot down my notes. Only later, when it was time to be Lady Macbeth, did it affect me.

Stuart rolled his eyes when I walked into the theatre.

"Everything good, Stu?" I asked. Out of the last three glorious weeks, he was the one blemish that existed.

"You've come in with a hangover," he said. "Last thing we need today."

"I'm not hungover," I said.

Stuart rolled his eyes again. "And you expect me to believe that? You look like death on legs."

"I'm not hungover. I've just got a bit of a cold." Honestly, I wondered what Ben was thinking about casting Stuart to play good King Duncan. There was nothing good about Stuart; he was tepid as an actor at best.

"You've got the plague if you're sick. No one looks that ghastly with a cold."

I had managed not to overthink about the Plague Doctor in the last three weeks. Of course, there were a few nightmares, but I refused to dwell on them when the morning came. And during those awful times when I woke with my heart pounding, I would distract myself by reciting my lines. Sure, was it any wonder that I was the first to have my lines down?

Margaret and her fluffy red cloud walked into the room. "What's this about the plague?" she asked. "Were ye watching the documentary last night?"

"This one, this murderous queen claims she isn't hungover but has the plague."

"I've got a cold, not the plague," I said.

"Are you bullying again?" Margaret scolded Stuart. "Just as well as you aren't a king, or you'd have us all roped and burnt."

There was no use in letting Stuart know that he had gotten to me, but he had. I went to the bathroom and checked my reflection in the mirror. I was pale, dreadfully so. But it wasn't uncommon. I wasn't someone who tanned. I didn't even freckle. I left the bathroom. It was damp and stuffy in there and was doing little to ease the tightness in my chest. At the end of the steps that led to the bathroom, there was an emergency exit that fed out onto an alleyway. It was here that the smokers gathered whenever they had a few minutes to spare. I propped the door open with the brick that was kept there for that purpose and stood outside. There was a box for cigarettes screwed onto the wall, but few used it, judging by the confetti of filters on the wet ground. Around me was an abundance of graffiti on the walls and an empty bottle of vodka sitting like a guard in the middle of the alley. It wasn't the most tranquil of places to ease my anxiety, but the air (despite it smelling like smoke) did help, and a few breaths later, I felt better. Yet the November chill had made me even colder than I had been. I would need something hot to warm my bones. I walked up the steps and went into the kitchen.

Margaret was in there, standing by the boiling kettle.

"Don't let him get to you. He's got an arse where his heart should be." She wore dangly gold earrings. I'd always feared wearing earrings like that in case I got into a fight and someone pulled them from my ear. I couldn't imagine Margaret going around fighting with anyone unless it was Stuart. He didn't pick on her, but she was ready to step in whenever she saw him riling up someone else.

I laughed at Margaret's joke. At least, I assumed she was joking, but truthfully I could imagine him with a miniature arse inside his chest. The kettle came to a boil, and its bright blue light turned off. Overhead, I could hear something being dragged across the floor. Perhaps this was the reason that the ceiling lights flickered.

"Are you having tea?" she asked. "Getting something warm into you would be good for that cold of yours."

"I would love a cup," I said. I rinsed one of the mugs in the press and filled it with tea.

"Here's to a great rehearsal." Margaret held her mug in the air and tilted it towards me. I clinked my mug, nothing special—white and chipped—against her cauldron mug.

"I hope it will be," I said.

"It will," Margaret said.

She was wrong though. At least for me, it wasn't great. Nothing awful happened. Everyone else had a smooth rehearsal. Only Daniel forgot his lines from time to time, but I was there to whisper them to him. I'd no trouble remembering my lines—of course, I didn't. But my delivery was poor, and my throat, which had only been a bit sore throughout the day, roared like fire so that any line I said sounded like a lacklustre frog had spoken it.

After a particularly bad moment when I had a coughing fit strong enough that I thought I'd vomit, Ben asked me if I needed to take a few minutes.

Stuart watched from the side of the stage. "See, you've cursed yourself saying what you said." He smirked at me with his arms folded across his chest. "Nothing good will ever come from saying that word."

"I haven't cursed myself." I was angry, but it was hard to sound it with a sore throat. I walked away and went back to the kitchen. This time, I added a spoonful of honey to my tea. I guess it sort of helped, for I was able to finish the rest of the rehearsals without any coughing fits. It didn't hurt either that I only had two more scenes left; I was mostly silent in them. After Lady Macbeth died, I sat at the side of the stage, watching the rest of the play.

When the rehearsal was over, Ben spent five minutes singing their praises. He included me, making sure to meet my eyes, but I knew I shouldn't be among the praise tonight. When everyone was trickling out, Ben came over to me and squeezed my shoulder. "How are you feeling now?"

Like death. Walking death. "I've felt worse," I said. "A good night's sleep, and I'll be right as rain."

"Good," he said. "Can you wait another twenty minutes or so? I've got to have a quick chat with Stuart."

"Stuart?" I groaned.

Ben knew my feelings for Stuart. It was no big secret. He laughed. "He wants to show me costumes in the attic. There's more of them stored up there. Apparently, they won't all fit in the storage room. Come with us if you like?"

I would prefer to cut off my hair than spend any more time with Stuart than warranted. "No thanks. I'll let you to it, and I'll go over my lines."

There was no one else around. If there had been, Ben wouldn't have kissed me. "Are you not afraid of catching my cold?"

"It's only a cold," he smiled. "Not the plague." There was that word again. I hated hearing it. I could only imagine how fearful of a word it was when the plague was going around killing everyone.

I watched Ben walk away before climbing onto the stage. Here, I had it all to myself. I mouthed my lines for the first ten minutes. It sounds silly, but I was feeling self-conscious. I wanted to make sure that everyone had gone home before I started. When the theatre was silent, and the only noises were the regular moans and groans that you would expect in such an old building because it was old, dating back to the mid-1800s, I cleared my throat and recited my lines. I only did one monologue before my sandpaper throat got the better of me.

Mam was not only dedicated to preventing sickness, but she was just as greedy for a cure. There was a drawerful of medicine back in the house, with at least a quarter of it containing remedies for a sore throat. As soon as I arrived home, I would ransack that drawer and take it to my bed. I was just about to leave the stage when I saw the movement way above in the gods. I thought it was Ben coming to watch me. I was wicked cute. First, I gazed out onto the stalls, fixing my eye on the very middle of the red seats. It was the one that I always stared out on, and I knew, even though I couldn't see it from here, that there was a small hole right in the top corner of the fabric. Next, I looked at the gold bar in front of the dress circle and then at the gods, where there were two gold bars. Despite the pain in my throat, I had a smile on my face, all ready for Ben. It wasn't Ben. The Plague Doctor stared down at me, hidden there in the shadows of the unlit gods. Its scythe was in its hand, and it raised the weapon as if in greeting.

I pinched the skin on my hand and closed my eyes. I am here. I am real. I am not imagining anything. Anything real will still be there when I open my eyes. Sure enough, it was. The Plague Doctor tilted its head. My phone was in my jeans pocket. I took it out and rang Ben, all the time keeping my eyes on the gods.

Ben's phone rang out.

I walked off the stage and went into the foyer. "Ben?" I called, my voice shaking. "Ben?" There was no hope I would be looking for him in the attic. I heard movement in the kitchen. "Ben?" I called again, keeping my footsteps light.

There was no one in the kitchen. The only thing in there was Margaret's cauldron mug upside down on the rack. I closed the door and flicked the switch on the wall. The light flickered. Just for a second, I kept my hand flat on the door. There was no lock—brilliant move on my part. My phone vibrated inside my pocket. I slid it out. Ben's name was on the screen.

"It's here," I said. "The Plague Doctor."

Ben sighed. "Are you joking with me?"

"No. I wish I was fucking joking, but I'm not." Scratching against the door. Followed by a thump. "It's outside the door," I said.

"Where are you?"

The doorhandle turned. "In the kitchen," I said.

"I'm on my way," Ben said.

The door pushed inwards. I flung my back against the wood. It was no use: I was no match. The door flung open, and I landed with a bang on the ground, hitting my head against the tiles. Then, it all went dark.

When I came around, Ben crouched before me. "Lacey?" he said. His hand was checking my neck—for a pulse, I could only presume.

I would've sat upright, but the pain in the back of my head was too intense. "The Plague Doctor, it was here."

Ben's jaw twitched. "The guards are looking around for it. And the ambulance is on its way."

The paramedics arrived shortly afterwards, shining a torch into my eyes, nearly burning my pupils in the process. Ben stood to the side, watching as I was lifted onto a stretcher. This was overkill. I told them there was no need for a stretcher, but when I had been pressed to stand earlier, my legs had given way, and I would've fallen if it weren't for the paramedics at either side of me.

"Stay with us now." The other paramedic, a woman with shoulder-length ginger hair, shone the light into my eyes. "No visiting lullaby land anytime soon for you. You'll have to have your dreams here."

"More like nightmares," I said.

Later, lying in triage, the same nurse who had tended to my injuries from my bike ride loomed over me. "Back again," she said. She had a thick Cork accent. Even though she was nothing like Jess, being petite and motherly, the accent reminded me of her, and I wanted to shove cotton balls into my ears.

"I am."

"What happened to you this time? Not going around without a helmet again?"

No one had told her then. That was good. I didn't want her to know what happened. She wouldn't believe it. You could tell by the look of her that she wouldn't believe it.

Ben came with the guards, standing in the middle of them like they were his bodyguards. "Hey," he said when he saw me. "How are you feeling?"

"I've been better," I said.

The Cork nurse had been informed that the guards wanted to speak with me before I was set free. I didn't know if she knew what they wanted because she kept giving me a funny look. "I'll leave ye to it," she said. She walked away with her hands in her pockets.

"I better go too," Ben said. "I'll be in the waiting area."

I nodded.

The tallest of the guards. A man with burnt orange hair and silvery eyebrows spoke first. "You've had quite the night," he said. "Mind if we have a little chat with you about it?"

The little chat lasted five minutes. I went through the

details of everything that happened, and the other garda, a grey-haired man with a stooped back, wrote notes.

"But this masked figure," the orange-haired garda said, "never actually tried to hurt you, did it? It was the bang on the head that put you in here."

"I don't think it was trying to get into the kitchen just to have a chat," I said. "And it's not the first time that this has happened either." I told them what happened on Halloween, leaving out the part Ben and I suspected I could've just had a huge fright. Now I know I was just gaslighting myself. Sometimes, believing your psyche was wilting rather than accepting the truth was easier.

The car ride home was mostly silent. Ben spoke only when we were nearing my parents' house. "Lacey, I've something I need to get off my chest. I know I'm going to sound like the biggest arsehole, but it might make you feel better."

I stared at him. "What is it?"

"Last week, I was talking with the lads, and I told them about what you thought you saw on the night Natalie died and how you thought you saw it on Halloween."

"What," I asked, sitting upright in my seat. "Why would

you tell them that?"

"We were watching an old horror movie on Netflix, and then we talked about ghosts and all that. I was just trying to explain how people can imagine things."

"I wasn't imagining things," I said. "I know what I saw."

"Tonight, I think you did see something," Ben said. "And if it's Gary, I'm going to fucking kill him."

"Gary. What does anything have to do with Gary?"

"He was there with the lads. He thought it was brilliant. He was mad to rip the piss out of you, only I warned him not to say a word, but you know what Gary's like. I bet whoever he told was the one wearing that costume you saw tonight."

Ben drove onto the street where I lived. Someone had already installed their Christmas tree in their front room, and its lights blinked at us as we drove past.

I stared at my hands. They were dry from the cold and the skin was red and peeling. "I can't believe you told them what happened," I said. "That was personal."

"I know," Ben said. "And as soon as I said it, I knew I had messed up. I wouldn't've said anything, only I was super drunk. I'm really sorry."

"Okay," I said. There was nothing else to say. "So, you think it was just someone trying to freak me out tonight?"

"Yes," Ben said. "And I'm going to kill whoever it was. Tomorrow, I'll organise a meeting with the cast and suss out who did it."

"Sure, if it was Gary, he could've told anyone. It doesn't mean it was anyone in the cast. Plus, I don't want everyone to know what happened. Can't you just look at the cameras?"

"Only the ones in the foyer are working," Ben said. "And I think whoever it was skipped the foyer altogether because the emergency exit door was open."

"I think I left it open when I went down there earlier for air." I could clearly remember opening the door but not closing it.

"Makes no difference," Ben said. "This was planned, and they must've been planning on going out that way anyway. That makes me believe it was someone in the cast, so they would know there were no cameras there."

I didn't know if this made me feel better or not. Was it better that some demonic entity was stalking me, or one of my cast mates was trying to terrify me?

"I bet whoever it was is feeling pretty shit now," Ben

said.

"It must have been Stuart," I hissed. "He's the only one with the issue with me."

"It wasn't Stuart," Ben said. "He was with me the whole time. He only left just before I called you back."

Ben pulled up outside of my house. Mam was peeping out of the window. She wasn't trying to be secretive at all. I knew she was in a heap; I had given her a brief rundown of what had happened. Her frantic reaction had led me to hang up the phone. She tried to call me ten times afterwards. I texted her, saying my head was banging and I'd talk to her when I got home. The truth was, my head was banging, and I wanted peace and quiet. "I better go in before she comes out."

"I'm sorry for saying anything," Ben said. "I never thought anyone would do this."

I nodded and left the car. I knew he was watching me walk up the garden path. The engine only started after I gave him a final wave and went inside.

November 30th

The video recordings in Draíocht were useless. The footage only showed me walking out of the auditorium with my false bravado stance, followed a few minutes later by Ben walking Stuart to the front door. I knew they wouldn't find it on the cameras as soon as Ben told me it had left through the emergency exit door.

Whoever *it* was, I had no clue. Gary swore it wasn't him and that he hadn't told anyone what Ben had told him. Ben's other friends claimed to be just as clueless and innocent as Gary. Ben was extremely apologetic, bringing me a big bunch of flowers and a box of chocolates to make up for his slip of the tongue.

I was back in the theatre two days later. It was like being in a murder mystery where everyone was the suspect, except no one had been murdered. Let it stay that way. I wasn't long there when Stuart walked in.

"I told you there would be a curse on the production, didn't I?" Stuart said.

"I reversed the curse," I said.

Stuart shrugged. "You might've done, but yet you still managed to maim yourself on two separate occasions. Are you usually this unlucky, madam?"

"Don't call me madam," I said.

"So, you aren't usually this unlucky," Stuart said. "I didn't think so. At least the curse seems to only be on you."

"Go away, Stuart," I said. "You're nothing but a pain."

Stuart chuckled, but he left me alone. I had a few moments of peace before Gary found me.

"Lacey," he said as if he hadn't seen me in years. "Could I have a word with you?"

"I suppose so," I said. The two of us went into the office. It smelled like Ben's cologne.

Gary closed the door and turned to me. "I swear to God I didn't say anything to anyone."

"Then it was you wearing the costume. Think it was

great fun tormenting me, did you?" I asked.

"I swear, it wasn't me." Gary had his hands in the prayer position. "I would never do that." Gary wasn't a great actor and had no business studying Theatre Studies. So, either he had suddenly learned how to act or was telling the truth. "There were other lads there. Two of them: Rasher and Leon. Either of them would've done it. I know what they're like."

Ben had already asked them. Both swore they hadn't done anything. Maybe they hadn't. If they told other people, then anyone might've tried to frighten me. It could've been anyone.

On the 30th of November, on a day when it was extremely cold and the roads were icy, Ben picked me up, and we went to the theatre together. Despite the cold, everyone was in good form that day. Everyone but me. All I could think about was who had been behind the mask. I was a ghost on stage that day, and even as I said my lines, my mind was far away. We were halfway through the play, and I was just about to leave the stage when I saw the figure standing to the side of the stalls. It was still buried in the shadows, but I could see the sharp point of its nose and its tall scythe that rose into the air. Instead of diving into the side of the stage, I walked down the three steps that brought me to the floor and cut across the room. The figure emerged from the shadows and came towards me.

Ben was to my left, talking to one of the cast members. I pressed my hand on his shoulder, urging him to turn around. He did, but by then, I knew. Evie had slipped out ten minutes earlier for coffee. I could see her coming in through the doorway with two bamboo travel cups. She grinned when she saw me. The figure was just in her eyeline now. She would be able to see it, but Evie made no sign that she had. She just kept walking.

"Are you good?" Ben asked. My hand was still on his shoulder. I let it drop. The figure was right there, only a foot away, staring at me. Evie didn't see it. She came over and presented my coffee to me.

"Lacey?" Ben whispered.

Before I could ask them to look at what they had been too preoccupied to see, the figure faded. Not that it ran away or dived back into the shadows. Let me make this clear: one moment, it was standing there, and then, as if it were steam, it drifted away into nothingness.

"Lacey?" Ben said, this time a little more harshly.

I looked at Ben and blinked. What could I say to him? Nothing that would make sense about what I had just witnessed. "I just," I shrugged, "nothing." I took the coffee from Evie and sipped it. I had asked for a latte, but she had added a caramel shot to it. She always did this like she wanted everyone to be as sweet as her. I thanked Evie and walked into the foyer. It was the first time I had walked anywhere by myself in the theatre all day. I was too afraid that whoever had been behind the mask would jump out at me again. But there was no one behind the mask—or nothing living. I was right all along. It had come through on the night of the Ouija board. It slipped into our world, and now it was stalking me and feeding on my fear. That was true, wasn't it? On the night I first saw it, I was terrified of that bloody board. Then, when I saw it on Halloween, I was still petrified. The last time I was spooked by the constant mentioning of the plague. Tonight, just before seeing it, I had been afraid again, thinking I had no idea who was behind the mask.

"Lacey?" Ben followed me out into the foyer. "You okay?" he asked.

"I'm grand," I said. I was. That thing wanted my fear. It wanted me to be afraid. I wouldn't give it that anymore.

That's what it fed on; now, I would make it starve. It masked itself with the plague, and I would mask myself with the famine.

December 10th

The Christmas lights were going to be turned on this evening. Ben and myself are heading into town to watch. There were lots of things happening, including a parade and street performers. That's not even mentioning all the food stalls there will be. I'd been thinking about going all day while sitting in the library in college doing my assignments.

Evie, Kim, and Dervla are going into town together tonight to watch the lights. "Want to be the fourth witch?" Dervla asked.

"I'm going in with Ben," I said. "We might catch you in there though."

"How sweet is that?" Dervla asked.

They all shipped Ben and myself. It was nice. What wasn't nice was the last two rehearsals. Ben was getting frustrated that half of the cast was still so shaky with their lines. I couldn't blame him. Opening night was New Year's Eve, and there weren't many rehearsals left, so everyone was busy. Even the ones that weren't in college had a ton of things to do. I could only hope they'd use that week off around Christmas and drill those lines into their heads. If not, then I'd be whispering lines to them on opening night.

When Ben called me that evening, you'd never think anything was stressing him. "Did you get your rose?"

"You sent me a rose?" I asked.

"Did you see the messages on WhatsApp?" he asked.

"No," I said.

"It would've been Natalie's 22nd birthday today," he said. "We're all meant to leave a red rose on her grave— they were her favourite."

I knew I was blushing crimson. I pulled the top of my turtleneck up a little to hide my face. "I haven't looked at WhatsApp today," I said. I had the group on silent. Maybe another reason they struggled to learn their lines is that they spent so much time messaging each other. Most of it was nonsense, not related to the Scottish Play.

"We were all meant to do it," he said. Ben smiled. "But no worries, one rose will do for the two of us. I figured since we're passing the graveyard on the way into town, we could just stop by?"

"Sounds great," I said.

We left my house. Mam was in the kitchen with the radio loud enough that she didn't hear Ben knock. If she had heard, she would've run to the door and asked him in for tea and a mince pie.

There was a tree air freshener in Ben's car. It stank up the place, making my stomach heave. Ben flicked it, and the tree swayed from side to side. "My annual Christmas car tradition," he said. "It smells just like the real thing, doesn't it?"

I nodded and smiled—no need to be rude when Ben looked delighted with himself. Ben put on Christmas music as he drove through town. Traffic was heavy, with cars lined up bumper to bumper. It took a solid twenty minutes to reach the graveyard. It was dark now at twenty past six, and the graveyard's gates were locking in ten minutes. I pointed this out as I opened the gate.

"We better not get locked in here then," Ben said. He

smiled at me mischievously. "Wouldn't want to meet anything creepy."

"I've enough of creepy in my life as it is," I said.

I knew we were thinking of the Plague Doctor. While he was thinking about which of his friends had either donned a mask or spilt the secret, I was gloating that my decision not to be afraid of the figure had kept it away.

"Are you calling me creepy?" Ben asked. "Because it's not my fault that my face looks like this."

"I think you have got a lovely face." He did, terrible taste in air fresheners but his face was beautiful. We kissed before walking to Natalie's grave. I hadn't been back since her funeral, but I knew it was at the left-hand corner on the second last row. It had been the last row on the day of her burial, but the dead need to be buried, don't they? The frosted earth over Natalie's grave looked a little pregnant. Flowers surrounded the wooden cross at the top of the grave.

"The lads are putting together a GoFundMe to get her a tombstone. The family are broke." Ben placed the rose onto the earth. There were six of them there already, all in their plastic wrappers. "I hope she's happy wherever she is."

"I hope so too," I said. It was bloody freezing now. I was terrible at wearing the right clothes for the season. I wasn't a huge fan of graveyards either. They always gave me the heebie-jeebies.

The first flakes of snow fell as we were leaving the graveyard. I dropped my head back and gazed at the white sky. A drop fell onto my nose, and I giggled. "Snow at last," I said.

"Maybe it's Natalie saying hi to us," Ben said.

I wish he hadn't said that. I didn't like the idea of Natalie watching us. Especially when I hadn't brought her a rose. More snow came. Enough that I had to stop looking at the sky, or else it would blind me altogether.

We went into the car. The heater was still toasty, and it came on as soon as Ben pulled out of the car park. I sat huddled up next to it. You'd think for such an awful perisher; I would cop on and wrap myself up. Maybe this would be the final lesson.

"Imagine if we got snowed in the car," Ben said. "That would be mad, wouldn't it?"

"Don't say it, or else you'll make it come true," I said. "At least not in the car. If we're going to get snowed in, then let it be somewhere with a fire."

"I could put a fire video on YouTube?" Ben said.

"It would do until the battery ran out," I said.

I was much warmer now. It was lovely sitting inside the car, watching the snow fall and the people twirling around in it. What should've been a five-minute drive into town took fifteen, and there were another five minutes of searching through the car park for a space, but eventually, we found one. We left the car. It was even colder outside now with the snow swirling. Away from the graveyard, I didn't mind the cold. It was different here, surrounded by so many of the living. There was a great joy in the air and the thrill of life buzzing. Even when the snow stopped, it didn't stop people from grinning.

Ben and myself wandered around town. I bought a red woolly hat and matching gloves, and with the two of them on, I didn't feel so cold anymore. We bought hot chocolate and drank our drinks by the giant Christmas tree in the middle of the square. Evie, Dervla, and Kim found us here.

"I love your hat," Evie said, running over to us. "Red's your colour."

Red was my colour.

Kim had on red gloss that day. There was the tiniest blob of it on her teeth. "Speaking of red," she said, "did ye leave your roses on Natalie's grave?"

"Just back from it," Ben said. "It started snowing when we were up there."

"I hope it starts again," Evie pouted.

"Me too," Dervla said. She touched her gloved hand against my own. "I was in Cork yesterday with my Mam, visiting my aunt and doing a bit of shopping." She stared, waiting for me to say something.

"That's nice." Although I couldn't imagine why she thought this would interest me.

"The line isn't bad now," Ben said. His eyes were on the little red food truck with the overpriced but delicious doughnuts. "Will we go over?"

"You go," Dervla said, "Lacey is okay with us." She tilted her head, showing far too much of her already upturned nose. She continued, not even looking at Ben. "Guess who I saw there?" There was no time for me to guess before she said, "Jess."

Evie glanced at the time on the grey clock tower nestled between colourful buildings. "Oh, we better get moving, or we'll be late. We're going to the cinema. Dervla wants to see that new Christmas film."

"I don't mind watching the parade instead," she said.

"You didn't say that earlier," Kim said. She had a tube of lip gloss in her hand, which she opened and applied as Evie took her arm.

"And we've tickets for the cinema." Evie linked Dervla with her free arm, said goodbye, and walked away. Then, it was just Ben and myself. He looked happy to see them go.

"Weird sisters by name, just plain weird by nature," Ben said.

I thought of the warning from Madam Lee. I still believed it was about Jess—only it was a shame Madam Lee couldn't have been a little clearer. If I had known to stay away from Jess, there's no hope I would've gone near the Ouija board, and that entity wouldn't have stuck with me. I would've saved myself from so much hassle. Still, at least I knew now.

"You alright, Lacey?" Ben asked.

I was staring off away, and I caught a glimpse of myself in a shop window straight across the way. I had the sometimes-vacant look of Evie. "I'm all good. Will we get these doughnuts then?"

"We will," Ben said.

We strolled over, bought the share-size box, and ate

them in front of the Christmas tree. From there, we watched the parade pass us by. It was longer than it had been any other year, with a marching band dressed up like Nutcracker dolls and a variety of street performers. Then, there was the man himself on his sleigh.

I looked up at him in awe, smiling away to myself.

"I hope I don't have any competition, do I?" Ben asked. He squeezed my hand, and I kissed him.

When the parade was over Ben and myself stayed in town for a little bit, walking around until finally, I had to admit defeat to the cold, and we went back to the car. It was a great evening. I was alive with Christmas cheer and wonder. There's nothing like some of that Yuletide joy to rid all of the horrors of the last few weeks.

"I'll see you tomorrow," I said to Ben before leaving his car. It still stank but my stomach wasn't as queasy sitting in it now.

"You will," I said. "Hopefully, rehearsals go better tomorrow than the last time," I said.

"They can hardly go any worse, can they?"

"Unless I forget all of my lines," I said. "That would be worse."

Ben laughed. I watched him drive away before I opened

the gate and walked up the garden path. The parents were in the sitting room watching an old Father Ted episode that they had seen a hundred times before, but they were still laughing away at it. There was an electric fire covering the front of the fireplace; the light was on, giving off a tangy orange colour, but no heat was emitted from it.

"We got your snow; did you see it?" Dad asked.

"I did," I said. "It was beautiful."

I sat with them for a few minutes. We had one of those plastic protectors on our sofa. I think we were the only people with one of them anymore. It made crinkly sounds as I snuggled deeper into the sofa. The Scottish Play was on top of the mantle; I had left it there just before leaving the house to meet Ben. When I had enough of watching Father Ted, I stood up and retrieved the play.

"Ah, Lacey," Dad said. "Would you ever give it a rest for one night? There's not a bit you don't know already."

"He's right, Lacey," Mam said.

I had read the play over and over. I was afraid that if I didn't, I'd forget my lines, and on opening night, I'd stand there on the stage like a big silent dummy. But I was tired. Sleep and myself hadn't been getting on so well recently. "Maybe I'll just get an early night." It was still only half nine, but I was so behind on sleep that it couldn't do me any harm. If I couldn't sleep, I'd come back downstairs and get the play. I said all this with such bravado, but in my head, I saw myself on the stage in a terrifying silence.

"The best thing I've heard you say in ages," Mam said. I guess she meant well, but even if she meant well, she could only give backhanded compliments.

"Goodnight then," I said.

The two of them wished me goodnight, and I went upstairs. I took off my makeup. My skin was red and chaffed from the cold. I smothered it in cream and got into my pyjamas. I had just put a relaxing ambience on when I got the text message from Ben telling me it was snowing again. I jumped out of bed and looked out the window. It was snowing. Flakes of it fell from fat clouds that were visible even in the dark night. But it was the Plague Doctor standing underneath the streetlights that got my attention. I closed my eyes. I wasn't afraid. When I opened them, it was gone, and all was right with my world.

December 22nd

I am proof that if you believe in something enough, it will become real. I believed I wasn't afraid. I refused to be afraid, and it's been twelve days since I saw the Plague Doctor. I guess it helped too, with how busy I've been. I've done all of my assignments and handed them in.

There was just one more exam to do. It was on at two, and I had been up at 5 a.m. to study for it. I would've stayed home and studied there, but Mam was in one of her moods and was making a racket downstairs. So, at nine, I left the house and walked to the Main Campus. There was no hope of me bringing my bike now with all the glittering ice on the roads—all that glitters is not golden I can tell you. I put on my earphones and jammed to my Christmas Spotify mix until my battery died halfway on my walk. Normally, I hated walking without music, but it wasn't so bad. Without music keeping me in my head, I noticed the Christmas décor around me and the quiet winter beauty.

When I reached C.T.U., I went straight to the café in the library and bought a hot chocolate. Then I went downstairs to where all the Arts students sat. I'd usually always sit by the window, but my seat was taken. After a quick walk through the library, I saw the whole place was packed. I left, cradling my hot chocolate against my chest. There were a few seats upstairs, but the place was too busy for me to get any decent amount of studying done.

"Hi, Lacey." It was Evie, she had on elf ears that jingled as she ran over to me. "One more exam," she said. "How brilliant is that?" Gary followed over. He had no elf ears, but he made just as much noise with the way he was dragging his feet.

"It's great," I said. "I'm excited for some relaxing time."

"You won't be doing much relaxing with Ben around," Gary said. He smiled at me lecherously.

"Well, we'll relax, won't we?" Evie asked. "Have a girls' night or something. It would be good for us to talk."

"That would be nice." A freezing gust of wind blew past

us. Today, I wore one of my proper winter coats, but the wind crawled underneath and slapped at my skin. I eyed the business building. It was always the place that I went to if the library was either too loud or too busy.

"I'll see you both later," I said. "Maybe we'll even go for a drink after the exam?"

Evie nodded so fast that I feared her head might fall off.

"Sounds cool," Gary said.

I watched them walk over to the library. They'd probably sit upstairs; I don't think they would be overly distracted by the abundance of noise. I guess I was just sensitive like that. I went over to the large building at the edge of campus. It was all shining glass outside, and it reminded me of an iceberg.

Despite it being the Business Building, we usually had one class here a semester due to a problem with room schedules. I pushed my way through the revolving door and entered the lobby. There was a massive Christmas tree with twinkling lights on the left-hand side. In front of it were two leather sofas with a handful of students reading over notes. In the middle of the building was a staircase with a glass surround. I climbed up it. After I had scaled the stairs, I was well and truly warm.

At the end of the second year, we studied Gothic Literature with the English majors. The class was held in a room at the back of the corridor. It was smaller than what it should've been for thirty students, but it didn't matter all that much since there was rarely even a third in attendance. I liked it and had spent many happy hours sitting next to the radiator watching the cold wind blow outside. I went in there, happy that the radiators were still piping hot. I plugged my phone in at the back of the room so I wouldn't be distracted. Then I took my usual seat and started studying.

I had two essays prepared for the exam. Sometimes, I would learn them word for word. I probably could've done it now, but I was too fearful of tampering with the lines that were already in my head. Instead, I read my bullet points and memorised my references. When it was time to leave, my hand was sore, but I felt good. There was little anxiety, knowing that I had done my best to prepare for the exam.

I left the room. The doors were all closed upstairs, but I could still hear the wind rattling them. That was the payment for being on the third floor, I guess. I walked down the stairs. A few people were sitting on the couches next to the large Christmas tree in the lobby. I crossed over the path and went to the sports building where our exam was on. Evie stood outside. Gary was no longer with her, but Dervla, Kim, and Marcus were.

"Everyone ready?" I asked. My teeth chattered in the cold.

"If being ready is the certainty that I'll fail," Evie said, uncharacteristically pessimistic.

"Of course, you're not going to fail," I said. "I bet you're more ready than any of us."

"I just have this strange feeling," Evie said.

"What kind of feeling?" I asked.

"That something's going to go wrong." Evie shrugged. "I guess if I fail, I can always repeat. Not the end of the world, right?"

"None of us are going to fail," Dervla said. "None of us. But we are going to have to go inside and do the test. Life's all about tests, isn't it, Lacey? You can take them to be positive or negative. Or turn something negative positive."

I didn't have a clue of what she was talking about. I saw Evie shoot her a dirty look and thought they'd been smoking something. It wouldn't be the first time. We all went into the building. We left our bags and coats in the hallway. The exam doors were already open. The sports hall was filled with rows and rows of tables and chairs. I liked to sit at the back and watch everyone. You'd know the first years who were bound not to return after the Christmas break. They were the ones who would reek of alcohol or who would attempt their exams for ten minutes before laying down their pen and waiting for the first hour to pass so they could leave the hall—other years tended to care more and more until finally there were those in their final year who had the reek of seriousness about them. Maybe that was the reason for Evie's sudden exam anxiety. I gave her the thumbs up as I sat down and then waited patiently for the exam to start. When it was time, I turned over the sheet. I couldn't've asked for better questions. What I had prepared for had come up. I glanced at Evie. She was smiling. I took a drink of water and wrote my references lest they slip from my head, and then I began writing my essays.

If I thought my hand was sore earlier, it was in agony when the bell rang, announcing that the exam was over. I flexed my hand, this way and that. There was even a red welt where the pen had been resting between my fingers.

A woman in her sixties, with a pink fringe and small gold hoops, took my paper. All my exams were over now.

There was no hope that I wouldn't go to the pub and have a celebratory drink. It would be criminal not to. I left the hall and joined the rest of my classmates outside.

Gary was about the only one who looked ashen of face. "I'm going to need to go on spirits to get over that one," he said.

"You'll be fine," Evie said. "I just know that you will."

"Easy for you to say. I saw you writing away," he said. "I just froze."

A group of us walked over to the campus pub. There was a gaudy Christmas tree in the middle of the pub on which several people had hung their bras. There might've been Christmas music playing on the speakers, but it was difficult to tell with how loud everyone in the pub was.

I joined Evie at the bar. She didn't say anything, just stared at the rows of bottles on top of the counter. It was no wonder she was quiet: we were all burned out and needed rest. The barman came to me, and I ordered cider. I always paid for everything with a tap of my phone. Only when I went to pay, and the phone wasn't in either my coat or my bag, did I realise it wasn't there. I knew where I had left it though. I could see it charging at the back of the room in the Business Building.

I left the pub and its noise behind and walked across the campus. All of the trees were long bare now, and their branches looked angry against the backdrop of the darkening sky. Above the setting sun was a line of straight red. Even the sky was joining in on the Christmas spirit.

In the Business Building, there was no one sitting on the sofas around the Christmas tree. They had finished their exams and were either in the pub or on their way home. I always wished I was one of those people who got to have that driving home for Christmas experience. I'd have it next year, though, if I got the opportunity to do my Masters in Dublin. Although being crammed in a bus to Castlebridge wouldn't be all that fun.

I walked upstairs. With no one in the building, my footsteps were even louder now. It was a wonder it was still open. The exam that I had just sat was the final one scheduled. At some point very soon, this building would close, and it wouldn't open again until January. I didn't want to be stuck here when it closed, so I picked up my speed. Above me, the chained light flickered as it swung with the sheer force of the wind. Inside the room, my phone was still plugged in, now reading 100%. I unplugged the phone, put it and the charger into my bag, and left the classroom. Another door, one very nearby, slammed. A doorway at the end of the corridor fed onto the fire exit stairs. We weren't meant to use it, but I had a couple of times.

I walked towards the main staircase, all the time staring at the fire door behind me. Only when I heard the heavy thump on the floor did I look in front of me. The Plague Doctor was at the top of the stairs. It stared at me with its head tilted to the side. In its hands, like always, was the scythe. My heart jumped, and my eyes blurred. Despite my earlier refusal to feed it my fear, I was scared. Scared enough, I turned around and ran as soon as my vision cleared. It chased me. Time slowed. I swear I had only taken a few steps, and in those few steps, my bravery kicked in once again. No way would I let it get the better of me. I stopped running. My trainers skidded on the floor. And I turned around and tackled it. I imagine if there hadn't been a mask covering its face, the shock would've been evident on it. My hands reached for the mask, but somehow, they were on the shoulders, pushing. Just that one push was all it took, and the Plague Doctor flew over the railing.

I clutched onto the top bar and looked over. It wasn't

the Plague Doctor who lay in a pool of blood on the ground floor; it was Evie.

"Evie," I whispered. Downstairs, I heard footsteps and excited voices. This was followed swiftly by a shrieking cry. I walked away, keeping my footsteps soft. I opened the emergency exit door and treaded softly down the stairs. The emergency door fed out onto the side of the building. If I followed the curved path, I'd arrive back at the pub. If I kept going straight across the frosted-over grass, I'd come to the road that led home. I crossed the grass. When I was on the road, I took out my phone and left a message in the Theatre Studies WhatsApp group saying that I would call it a day and go straight home. No one responded to it.

The next message came from Gary, saying that Evie had fallen down the stairs in the Business Building; she was alive but not in a good way. By this stage, I was at home sitting in my bedroom with a cup of tea in my shaking hand.

Alive! Evie was alive. I stared at my phone. The messages came in fast and hard on WhatsApp. I messaged, saying that I had just been in the Business Building and must've missed her.

Gary was on the phone with me twenty seconds later.

He was crying. I stared at my reflection in the mirror as I spoke to him. Why wasn't I crying? If Gary could, then shouldn't I be able to cry? Maybe it was a shock.

"Some young one studying Marketing found her. They think she tumbled down the stairs. You know what Evie's like, running everywhere. She probably saw you were gone and ran back to the pub. Not that this is your fault in any way, got that, Lacey? It's not your fault."

I nodded at my reflection. It wasn't my fault. It really wasn't.

December 24th

Evie was in a coma. I'd stayed in my room staring at my phone and watching messages appear on the screen. We all wanted to visit her but agreed it would be best to give her family privacy. So, we sent a humongous card with our signatures on it, as well as a dozen inflatable balloons. Evie would love them all, but I doubted the staff in the hospital will. I wanted to tell someone about what happened. I'd debated going to the guards, but what good would that do? No one would believe that an entity messed with my head and made me confuse Evie for it.

Mam knocked on my bedroom door and came in with a cup of tea and a pack of biscuits. She left them both on the bedside table.

"How are you feeling?" she asked me.

"Terrible," I said. "All that I can think about is Evie."

"The poor girl. And so close to Christmas too. I imagine her family must be in a heap." Mam sat on the seat in front of my desk. "Such a tragedy."

"She's not dead," I said.

Mam fidgeted in her seat. "It's rare for someone to fall from that height and survive, though, right? That she's in a coma is a miracle."

"Sure, you love your miracles," I said.

"I hope she will get one further and pull through." She smiled at me. "Will you drink your tea?"

"It's not spiked, is it?" I asked.

Mam laughed too loud. "Go way out of that."

I drank some of the tea and ate a ginger nut biscuit. I hadn't been able to taste food recently, but I could taste the ginger, which reminded me too much of Christmas. I left the rest of it half uneaten on the table.

Mam was looking at her hand in the way that she did whenever she had something that she wanted to say but wasn't sure how it would go down. "It's just as well that the play won't be on anymore. It has brought nothing but trouble. First, with your accident and then that eejit in the mask, now poor Evie in a coma."

I hated how she called her poor Evie; it reminded me of poor Natalie. "I don't know if the play is called off. Ben hasn't mentioned it to me."

"You'll have to know soon," Mam said. "The play is on in a week."

I didn't say anything to that. Later that night, people on the Scottish Play's WhatsApp group began to wonder the same thing as my mother. Eventually, it was Gary who told us that Ben was still deciding what to do.

December 26th

Christmas came and went. Evie was still in a coma. Ben texted me once on Christmas Day to wish me a Happy Christmas. I texted him, asking how his Christmas was going, but he didn't respond. This morning, he texted saying he had drank way too much and fell asleep while watching *Raiders of the Lost Ark*. The same movie had been playing while I sat with my parents and stared numbly at the television. Mam and Dad wore paper crowns on their heads and ate Quality Streets as they spoke through the movie. All I could think about was Evie in her hospital bed.

The tin of sweets was all gone when I poked my head into the sitting room. But the two of them were still sitting there glued to the screen.

"I'm off," I said.

"Where are you going?" Mam asked.

"Meeting Ben," I said. "We're going for a drive."

"That's nice," Mam said. "I'd say he'll let you know if the play is going ahead." She was just as obsessed with the outcome as the cast. I knew Mam was only fretting because she didn't want the play to go ahead. I think the rest of the cast wanted to continue, but no one would dare to admit it. I wasn't sure what to feel. Maybe Mam was right, and the play should be parked.

Ben looked wrecked, and he wasn't lying about overdoing it the night before, for there was the rank of alcohol steaming off him. "Hey," he said through a yawn. There was no kiss.

"You don't look great," I said. "Hope you're not sick?"

"Are you afraid you'll catch it?" Ben asked. "Because this sickness is because of my cousin Jack Daniels."

"Just as I thought," I said. I went to touch his hand, and it was cold. He pulled free from my hold and scratched his nose. He could pretend he'd an itch all he wanted, but I knew a snub when I saw one. "Everything okay other than the hangover?"

Ben pulled out, and we drove down the road. "Apart

from Evie being in a coma, life is flying."

"I'd no idea that you and Evie were so close." I kept my eyes on him. He kept his eyes on the road.

"Everyone likes Evie," he said. "What's not to like?"

"She's wonderful," I said. "I hope she will be just as wonderful when she wakes up."

Ben gave me the side eye. "You think she will wake up then?"

"I hope so," I said.

Ben wore the same clothes I had seen him wearing a few days ago. It wasn't a big deal, but it didn't look like the black jeans or shirt had been washed. "You don't seem yourself," I said.

Ben laughed. "How should I act when Evie could die? Shouldn't you be more upset, considering she's your best friend?"

"Evie's going to be fine," I said. "I know she will." We drove past the college; it was lonely and desolate looking on the grey December day. "Where are we going anyway?"

"Just for a walk," he said. "A bit of air will help clear my head."

"Couldn't we walk nearby?" I asked. "Go in for some coffee too?"

"I need some nature," he said. "And it's not far away."

Ben drove us to the outskirts of town. There was a walkway here that had only opened in September. I'd always been threatening to visit, but I never did. There was also a little coffee van with fairy lights on its roof. We joined the queue in front of it. After we got our drinks, we went for a walk on the path with views of the river that were still beautiful even on this miserable day.

"Sorry, I'm not myself," Ben said. "I've lots on my mind."

"Want to talk about it?" I drank from my latte. It was gingerbread; I don't know why I ordered such a festive drink when I just wanted it all to be over.

"Just worrying about what to do about the play, mostly. I'm thinking of Evie too—what happened to her was so tragic."

"It was tragic," I said.

"Mad for her to just fall like that, wasn't it? You would never hear of it."

Ben tried to take my hand, but this time, I pulled away.

"You're not mad at me for being grumpy, are you? I don't mean to take it out on you." He looked exhausted and hungover.

"No," I said. "I'm not mad." I took his hand and dropped it a minute later when we had to walk single file through the narrow exit that led to the river.

Ben drank from his Americano like it was Dutch courage and said: "I think the play should go on. I've been grappling with that. I feel awful about poor Evie, but I think it's what she'd want."

"Who would replace her though?" I asked.

"I have someone who already offered," Ben said.

"It's not Stuart, is it?" I asked.

Ben laughed. "No, it's Anna. I think a part of her was happy to have the extra lines."

Anna played Lady Macduff. She barely spoke—at least not to me. Ben and myself didn't walk for long before he dropped me home. There was a kiss but only a peck. That was okay. I didn't feel like kissing him much either.

That evening, Gary announced that the play would continue and that Ben would contact us later. Everyone was ecstatic—even I, despite my unease and fear for poor Evie.

December 28th

On the 28th of December, we met in the theatre for our first proper dress rehearsal. Unusual for Ben, he didn't bring me to the theatre. Instead, he asked if I could meet him there. I didn't mind, but I knew then that things were not right with us, but it didn't seem important when Evie was still in a coma.

Ben was talking to Stuart and Marcus when I arrived. The three of them waved at me from their place across the room. I returned the wave and went backstage. Kim and Dervla were there. They stopped talking as soon as I walked into the room.

"Everything okay?" I asked.

"We're just missing Evie," Dervla said. "It's such a

shame she went after you."

"It doesn't feel right without her here," Kim said.

"I hope I can do her justice," Anna said. I hadn't noticed her until that moment. She was sitting on a bench at the side of the room with the script open on her lap. "I really do." Anna was somewhere in her twenties. She had a high forehead with a small circular scar in the middle of it.

"You'll do great," I said. "I know Evie will be delighted it's you replacing her." I bet it was true too. But to be fair, I don't think Evie would mind who filled her shoes as long as someone did. She would hate for the play not to go on.

Stuart, done talking to Ben, came backstage. He saw Anna reading through Evie's lines and shook his head. "I knew this play was cursed. Once she said that word, I knew we were doomed."

As if sensing Stuart causing trouble, Margaret joined us with her hair, which looked surprisingly tame today. "The play isn't cursed. Evie had an accident. Nothing more and nothing less." Her eyes met mine, and she smiled. I had never been so grateful to be on the receiving end of a smile in my life.

Stuart rolled his eyes and wedged himself between Dervla and Kim. Kim mostly spoke to Anna, but I could see Stuart and Dervla taking sneaky looks at me. Margaret kept to my side, trying to engage me in small talk, but my mind was swirling again, thinking of that bloody curse and Madam Lee's words. Yet when it was time to go on stage, all my worries slipped away, and I could only be Lady Macbeth.

Ben watched from the front row. He was still pale and hungover looking, but at least he had changed his clothes. He hadn't appeared hopeful when the play began, but when it was over, he was beaming.

"Lads," he said. "That was spotless. If ye can keep that up, you'll get an ovation each night." We performed well; I agree with Ben there. But the performance wasn't perfect. Some people had forgotten their lines, and either me or another actor would have to whisper it to them. Other people had tripped over their words—I was even guilty of that myself on several occasions. But we got through it better than I had anticipated we would. We had two more dress rehearsals before opening night. Whatever mistakes we made tonight would just have to be ironed out then. I hoped.

After rehearsals, we were all meeting in The Player's Inn for a quick drink. I didn't feel much like attending. It felt wrong with Evie in the hospital, but I couldn't say no when everyone else was going. They had all gotten out of their costumes at rapid speed while I was still undressing. When I was fully dressed, I heard the scratching. I turned around, slowly, slowly. It was there in the middle of the doorway, scratching its scythe against the unplastered walls. The same red-hot anger filled my veins as to when this thing had made me push Evie over the bannister. I yelled and ran after it. It turned around and ran away down the narrow stone corridor and up steep stairs.

Just before I turned the corner, I saw the door to the third floor shut. I ran in here. At the back of the room, a floor-to-ceiling window let in light from the streetlight outside. It illuminated the Cinderella-like dress on the mannequin in front of the window. I palmed the wall until I found the light switch. I flicked it, and the room lit up. The place was dusty and filled to the brim with a million objects and costumes from hundreds of productions. In the middle of the room, pushed up against the wall, were three huge wardrobes. The door on the wardrobe in the middle vibrated.

There was no sound in the room. Even my heart seemed too still. I wondered if I was dead and if this was some peculiar version of the afterlife. I walked softly to the wardrobe. Before I could even touch the handle, the door swung open.

Tucked between a green dress and bright red pants was a long coat. Attached to the coat was the Plague Doctor's mask. I touched the coat, and it swung on the hanger, directing my attention to the scythe standing in the corner of the wardrobe.

"Lacey?" I could hear Ben calling me from downstairs.

"Lacey Lane, girl," Gary added. "We're all dying of the drought. Will you come on?"

I turned around and saw the plague doctor standing there. Icy cold mist smoked from its mouth and enveloped me.

I was no longer in the theatre but in a small living room with purple walls and an Ikea sofa with three skull cushions. On the coffee table were two glasses of vodka and coke. One of them only had a dash of vodka in it, while the other one was a brownish colour—only Jess drank her vodka like that. And it was here in Jess's flat that we were. The door leading to the sitting room opened, and Jess and Natalie walked out. In Natalie's hand was the Plague Doctor's outfit. In Jess's was a pack of tarot cards.

"You're sure you don't mind me keeping this costume?" Natalie asked with just a hint of an accent.

"It's my present to you for being my model." Jess sat on the sofa and picked up the lighter-coloured drink.

Natalie joined Jess on the sofa, leaving the plague doctor costume on the edge of the sofa. She touched the mask and swirled her fingertip around the design on the top. "This is very beautiful. Even more so when I know that you've hand-painted it."

Jess laughed. Her hair was freshly washed, and the curls were in a perfect corkscrew, not in the frizzy state that they usually were. "You think a plague doctor's mask is beautiful?"

"I do," Natalie said. "Very beautiful."

Jess shuffled the tarot cards in her hands. "Now, are you ready for your reading?"

"I was born ready," Natalie said. She moved her head, and her hair swished against her back.

Natalie put on the mask. "I'll store it upstairs in the theatre until I move to my new flat next week."

"You could just leave it here," Jess said.

"It's safer in the theatre than in your messy room," Natalie said. "Plus, this way it will steep in the theatre *energy. Now, are you going to read my cards?"*

A flash of bright light. And now Natalie was in the empty foyer. She held a black gym bag in one hand and the scythe in the other.

"Ben?" she called.

Ben's voice came from somewhere in the theatre. "Be with you in a moment."

"Make it five," Natalie said. She walked into the auditorium, went backstage, and climbed the steep stairs until she arrived on the third floor. Natalie entered the storage room. She went straight to the wardrobe and opened the door. She removed the black coat from the bag, hung it on a hanger, attached the mask to the front of the coat, and placed the scythe at the back of the wardrobe.

The vision, if you want to call it that, ended. Mere inches separated the Plague Doctor and myself.

"Natalie?" I asked. "Is that you?" My hands rose. My fingers were stiff as I went to pull off the mask. My fingers caught icy cold air, and the figure faded. When she reappeared, the mask was gone. That face, with its perfect bone structure, was deathly white. There was not a sign of decay on it, but there were a few specks of vomit around her bee-stung lips. I guess it was the eyes that did it. They had never looked at me friendly, but now there was only hate.

"Natalie," I said. "I'm so sorry about what happened to you." I stepped closer to her, and freezing air wrapped around me. There was cold, fear, and emptiness, and then Natalie was gone.

I left the storage room and went downstairs.

Ben and Gary were in the lobby. Ben still looked exhausted, but he gave a half smile when he saw me. "We were about to send out a search party," Ben said.

"I was just distracted by something," I said.

"How's a few drinks in the pub sound for a better distraction?" Gary asked.

"Not tonight," I said. "I'll catch ye the next time."

"Do you want a lift?" Ben asked. How he said it, I knew he wanted me to say no.

"I'd like the walk. It'll help me sleep tonight. I haven't been sleeping right."

Ben seemed happy enough with that. I said goodbye to the two of them and left the theatre, wishing I had never stepped foot into Draoícht. Now I knew for sure that Madam Lee's warning hadn't been about Jess. I was always meant to stay away from the play. Natalie hated me so much for taking her role that she had made me hurt poor Evie.

Outside shoppers were laden down with the bounty they had acquired in the 50% off sales. I stared at their faces. Most looked happy enough. The odd few looked sad, and one, like me, appeared to be in turmoil. Soon, I wouldn't feel this anguish; all I had to do was figure out how to stop Natalie. But maybe she would stop now. Maybe all she wanted was to let me know she was angry. Maybe, but I doubted it.

I was leaving the busy part of town when I saw a familiar face. She was so bundled up in a huge white winter coat, a green scarf, and a hat that I wouldn't have recognised her if those green eyes hadn't turned my way. She smiled distractedly as if trying to figure out who I was.

"Madam Lee," I said. I stopped walking. I don't think she wanted to stop. Her body was tilted in the direction that she had been walking before she relented and turned towards me.

"You have me at an advantage. You know my name, but I do not know what yours is."

"My name is Lacey, Lacey Lane. You gave a reading to me during the summer."

Still, Madam Lee didn't show any signs of recognition. "You were the girl who was wondering if she should go to America? I remember now." She touched my hand with her own. "Oh no," she said. "You're not."

"I'm not," I agreed. "You gave me a warning."

"Stay away from three witches. And you didn't. Did you?"

I thought of Jess and her Ouija Board and her band t-shirt that said Three Witches. "I thought it was my friend. I cut her off. I guess she wasn't what the warning was about."

"Evidently not," Madam Lee said.

Overhead, star-shaped Christmas lights twinkled. In one of the shops, Christmas music was still playing. I always thought playing Christmas music after December 25th should be illegal. "Do you have fifteen minutes? There's a little café over there. It's quiet, and I could use some advice."

Madam Lee had that slightly greenish look on her face again. "I have to get going," she said.

"I'm being stalked by the dead," I said. No matter how brave I had been earlier, fat, ugly tears flowed down my face now. "She was Lady Macbeth, but she died, and now she won't leave me alone." I gave up trying to be brave. I hadn't even cried for poor Evie, but now the tears were angry.

"Okay, okay," Madam Lee said. I think she wanted to hug me. Her arms were raised before she abruptly put them down. It looked strange and even a little funny. "Where do you want to go? I really can't stay long. I'm already past my meter time."

I led Madam Lee to a bookshop that overlooked the centre of town. A waiter with a French accent and thick sandy hair came and took our order. While we were waiting for our drinks to come, I told Madam Lee everything that had happened, starting with my visit to her and learning about the Plague Doctor's identity.

Our drinks came. Madam Lee looked as though her head was going to explode. She drank from her hot chocolate. "So, your friend wore a Three Witches top, and they're a band?"

I nodded.

"But you don't think the warning was about her now. You think it was about the play because of the misfortune that's followed you since?" she asked.

I nodded.

"And you believe that you're being stalked by the ghost of the woman who was meant to play Lady Macbeth." She held the hot chocolate in front of her chest as if it were protection.

"I am." Here I was puzzled, though. I had seen the Plague Doctor on the night of the Ouija board. How could I see Natalie's ghost before she even died? I asked Madam Lee this.

"You were using a Ouija Board. They can make a place in between spaces. Did ye do a protective circle?"

"I don't think Jess did," I said.

"Hmmm," Madam Lee rested her chin on her hand. "If the original Lady Macbeth—"

"Natalie," I said.

"I think since the room was already an in-between place and Natalie's death was a shadow in the air. That would explain what you saw."

I shivered. "So, she was dead even before it happened?"

"Well, if time isn't liminal, aren't we all dead and not yet born?"

A headache was coming on. "What can I do to get Natalie to stop following me?"

"Tell her that you're sorry she's dead. You haven't done

anything wrong by taking the part. Or perhaps you could make her some form of an offering."

"Roses," I said. I knew exactly what Natalie would want. "She loved, loves, red roses. I could leave them on her grave?"

"It's worth trying anyway." Madam Lee drank from her hot chocolate. I hadn't been paying attention to her drinking while we were speaking, and somehow, she had already drunk most of it. She opened her wallet and handed me a copper-coloured card that said Madam Lee, wonder, medium, and clairvoyant. Following this, there was a phone number, email, and Instagram name. "If that doesn't work, contact me, and I can talk to her for you. I'd go with you now to the theatre, but I am late." She stood and put on the big white coat.

"Thank you," I said. I felt lighter than I had done before. Madam Lee left the café. I watched her walk away before leaving.

December 29th

I wonder what would have happened if I stayed away from the Scottish Play. Would Natalie have haunted the new Lady Macbeth, or did she only stalk me because she had never been my fan to begin with? The worst part is that even if Natalie stalked the new Lady Macbeth, Evie would probably be okay.

If only Jess hadn't worn that bloody band T-shirt, I wouldn't be in this situation, and Evie would be okay. The only thing in my power now was to follow Madam Lee's suggestion and go to Natalie's grave. I dressed in black and went downstairs to the kitchen.

"There you are," Mam said. "You came in here last night without saying a word to anyone."

"I was just wrecked," I said. "I couldn't do anything but fall asleep."

"I know," Mam said. "I peeked in at you, and you were dead to the world. Where are you going? Looking like you're on your way to a funeral?" Mam's face went ashy. "It's not your friend, is it? Has something happened to her?"

I hadn't even thought about Evie since yesterday. "I haven't heard anything," I said.

"No news is good news," Mam said. "Unless they tell you that she's after waking up."

That would be the best thing that could happen today—that and knowing that Natalie had finally moved on. I said goodbye to Mam. She kept asking where I was going, so eventually, I told her I was visiting Natalie's grave. "I want to pay my respects to her one more time before opening night. It feels like the right thing to do."

"That's very good of you," Mam said.

I left the house, bought six red roses, and walked to the graveyard. I hoped the roses would be enough to pacify her. Jesus, I hoped that they would. There were few around in the graveyard. No surprise there. Only the hardiest of mourners would come out in this cold. I couldn't remember feeling the winter so much before, though it had more to do with Natalie following me than anything else.

Natalie's gravestone was now erected. I guess the GoFundMe had been a success then. It was a beautiful but simple tombstone with a picture of Natalie right in the centre of it. Her smiling eyes looked out onto the world of the graveyard. There was a little flower stand to the side of the tombstone with twelve holes to add flowers. I bet whoever bought it did so to keep roses in it. I unscrewed the top and checked to see if there was water in it. There was none. I refilled it and screwed the top back on, and then added the roses.

"I'm sorry that you're dead, Natalie," I said. There was no need to keep my voice low, for the other people in the graveyard were far away. "I wish that we had gotten to know each other better when you were alive, but there is no point in dwelling on that now. I am sorry that you never got to be Lady Macbeth. I know that you would've been great as her. I hope that you can move on now." I stayed quiet for a few moments—for me, the most peaceful form of prayer. Words are beautiful, but a lack of words can sometimes say so much more. When the tip of my nose slid into numbness, I left the graveyard. I hoped Natalie would leave me alone now.

December 30th

There was still no sign of Natalie. I guess my luck was changing. Not Evie's though. She was still in her coma. I was glad to have the Scottish Play to take my mind off Evie. Ben hadn't offered to bring me to the theatre again that day. I walked into town and found him standing in the lobby talking to Kim.

When I walked over to him, Kim whispered something into his ear and left.

"What was that all about?"

"What was what all about?" he asked with a sigh.

"You and Kim standing there like ye were conspiring," I said.

"She was just giving me advice about something," he

said.

His hair was dishevelled and getting curly now with the length in it. I didn't like his curls; they reminded me too much of Jess. I wished he would cut his hair off.

"I'm going to get a cup of coffee." He had a reusable cup with a picture of Shakespeare on it. "Do you want me to bring something back for you?"

"What's wrong with you?" I touched his sleeve, and he pulled away.

He closed his eyes. "I'm sorry. I'm just stressed with the show. It hasn't been an easy one." He touched my arm. "How about I bring you back something?"

"I'm okay," I said.

Ben nodded. "I'll see you inside in a few minutes. If everything continues as it has the last few days, then we'll have an amazing run."

The rehearsal did go well. It was the best performance that we had all given. There was no sign of Natalie either. Would it be too much to hope that she had taken my roses as a gift and wouldn't bother me anymore? I had hope. I would bring her the roses every fortnight just to make sure. Maybe it would be something my child and their children would continue to do for eternity, not knowing why, just accepting it as a family tradition.

Ben clapped for us after the performance and told us again how well we had done. He was all smiles, and his eyes glistened, but there was still something off about him. When I found him after everyone had cleared out of the theatre, he was in the kitchen drinking coffee. This time, it was instant and in a chipped red mug. When I got closer to him, I could smell the whiskey that he had added.

"Hey," I said.

His back was turned, and he jumped when he heard my voice. "Hey," he said, turning around. "You were wonderful tonight." I caught sight of my reflection in the mirror. I was still wearing my makeup. Fine for Lady Macbeth, but it made me look like a ghost in the kitchen.

"What's wrong, Ben?" I asked.

"Nothing's wrong," he said, his voice flat.

"Do you want to break up? Is that what this is? You don't need to wait until the play is finished to break up with me. I won't quit if that's what you're worried about."

Ben set his cup down on the worktop. "You'll want to break up with me when you hear." He took a deep breath. When he spoke again, the words were rushed, as if he had been holding them. "On the night of the fireworks, remember when you got drunk, and we couldn't find you?" he asked but didn't give me a chance to answer. "Jess and I split from Gary. We went looking for you outside. One thing led to the other." He drank from his mug. A long drink; he must've finished what was left in there. "Jess is pregnant. I only found out a few weeks ago." Ben scratched his head. "I didn't know what to do. I don't know what to do." He attempted to take my hand, and I shoved him away.

"You hate Jess," I said. "You told me you were delighted that we were no longer friends."

Ben sighed. "I'm still not a fan. I always knew she was an odd one, but I thought she could at least still keep her mouth shut. She had no business telling anyone, but she did. That is what makes it all the worse, Lacey. Who did fucking Jess meet in Cork but Dervla. Up doing her Christmas shopping, she was," Ben laughed. "Dervla's a mouth. I'd say that's why Jess told her. She probably wanted it to get back to you. And it would've got back to you sooner if Evie hadn't had her accident."

My head spun. I knew what was coming next. "She was coming to tell me, wasn't she?"

"Yes. Dervla swore her to secrecy. I'd say if it were about anyone else, Evie wouldn't have said a word, but you know how she is with you."

I did. Evie, my ever-faithful friend, and this was her reward for not keeping a secret. "If you had told me earlier, Evie would be okay."

Ben's jaw twitched, and something flashed in his eye. "It wasn't my fault she fell if that's what you're implying."

"I'm not implying anything, Ben. You didn't tell me, and now Evie's in a coma. It's your fault."

"I didn't want what we have going on to end."

"But it has anyways." I turned to leave the room. I was at the door when Ben called me back.

He looked scared when I came in, and now, he looked terrified. "And the play, will you still be Lady Macbeth?"

The absolute cheek of him. Did he think I'd ruin my role because of his mistake? "Yes." That's all he was getting out of me. Let him bubble away in his fear. Let him slowly simmer in it until he was dead—I didn't care.

December 31st

You know, if I were a cruel person, I would've given up on the Lady Macbeth role. I would've told Ben to feck off, and that would have been the end of our entanglement. No part of me wanted to do that. I was Lady Macbeth now. The two of us couldn't be separated. Even if we could, I'd never do that to the other actors, even Stuart. All of us had bled for the play. There were only three nights in the performance. When they were over, I would simply pretend that Ben didn't exist. Maybe in a year or so, I would see pictures of him and Jess's offspring on someone's Instagram. By then, I would be doing my Masters, and I wouldn't give a damn about the pair of them. All I had to do was give it my all for the three nights, and then I would get to the business of forgetting.

On New Year's Eve, our show was on at the early time of six o'clock—that way, if people wanted to go out that night, they would have time to see the Scottish Play first. The tickets were already sold out for the 1st and 2nd of January and sold out for the New Year's Eve show that very day. When I heard, the butterflies that hadn't existed in my stomach ran wild. Here I was in my first leading role. I didn't care about Ben's stupid mistake. I was the lucky one who got to be Lady Macbeth. He was the one who would always remain connected to Jess.

I was among the first to arrive at the theatre. Ben stood in the lobby. I knew he was waiting for me by the way his eyes lit up when he saw me. He had rung numerous times; not once did I answer his calls. "Hi, Lacey. I was worried you weren't going to show up."

"Well, I'm here." He kept on looking as I walked away. What did he expect that I'd just be okay after what happened? Maybe I could get over what he did with Jess, but he should have told me as soon as he found out.

Backstage, the weird sisters were huddled together. Kim and Dervla's blonde hair were nearly the same colour. I only noticed it there with their heads almost touching. They must've been talking about me before I entered the room because everything went quiet.

"You excited?" Dervla asked, smiling. She had some cheek to smile when she was also at fault for Evie's fall. I wonder how many people she told about that thing growing in Jess's stomach. She definitely told Kim anyway. That's what she and Ben had been conspiring about. I wonder what sage advice Kim had given him. Buy me some lip gloss before telling me?

"I am," I said.

Stuart joined us backstage. "Is everyone ready for the performance?" he asked.

"More than ready," Anna said.

It didn't seem right seeing her there where Evie should be. I wonder how many people looked at me like that and wished Natalie was in my seat.

Backstage filled up with the cast. We got into our costumes. Daniel was nervous—the worst of the lot of us. I could see him shaking. I hugged him and told him everything would be great and that he was a wonderful Macbeth. Ben walked in on us hugging, and he didn't look impressed. But he shifted his persona quickly, and he was back to being the star director, giving us a pep talk.

I didn't care for what he had to say anymore. My attention was focused solely on the buzzing filling the auditorium. The audience was arriving—my parents among them. Despite their many objections to me continuing my role, they were excited to see me in the play tonight.

Daniel disappeared for a few minutes. When he came back, he smelled sickly, and his face was pale. I couldn't help but think of Natalie. At least her ghost had stayed away. Poor Natalie.

Then, it was time to begin. I squeezed Daniel one more time, and he walked onto the stage, joining the three witches. Their scene flew past, and then it was my turn. There were so many lights. You'd think I'd be used to them now, but I wasn't. My eyes teared a little, but it didn't matter because I was excellent. For the whole show, I was excellent. When the standing ovation came at the end, it was for me. It wasn't for anyone else. But we bowed together, and I was happy to share the stage with the rest of the cast. I saw Natalie then. She still wore the black coat, but the mask was in her hand. She had a little smile on her face. She was happy for me. I welcomed the sight of her and blew her a kiss.

Backstage, we were all buzzing—every last one of us. I wouldn't share my joy with Ben. When he tried to hug me, I moved away, went in behind the dressing area's curtain, and got out of my dress. It wasn't long after then that Mam came and sought me out.

Ben led her to me. He was still grinning away.

"Mam, you shouldn't be in here," I said.

"You were brilliant," she said to me. She had a dozen red roses in her hand. "I know you love roses."

I did, but not blood red like Natalie's. I was gentle pink. "Thanks. But you shouldn't be in here."

"I need to talk to you," she whispered into my ear. I brought her into the hallway that led to the storage room upstairs.

"What's wrong, Mam?" I asked. "Is something the matter with Dad?"

"He's fine," she said.

"What is it then?" I asked.

"The guards called for you just before we left," she said.

I dropped the roses onto the ground. I heard the plastic scratch on the tiles, and then I picked them up. "Did they say what they wanted to talk to me about?"

"No," Mam said. "But I told them you were here. And I

saw them standing by the big stairs in the foyer when your play was over. Oh Lacey, are you in trouble?"

"You told them I was here?" I asked incredulously.

"I did," Mam said. "What else could I have done? What happened, Lacey? Did you do something?"

I heard the familiar scratching sound. She hadn't been standing there before, but Natalie was on the stairs now. One hand was on her scythe, and the other held her mask. There was a smirk on her face.

"You bitch," I said, my eyes were on Natalie's.

"What have you done?" Mam asked. She followed me as I left the hallway, walked through the backstage area, and then out through the auditorium. The guards were in the foyer but not standing by the stairs; they were by the front door talking to Ben. Mam's hand gripped my shoulder. I shrugged it off and made for the stairs. Mam might have followed me, but she couldn't keep up. Before I reached the top of the stairs, she had already given up the chase. But the guards stormed towards me.

I went all the way to the gods. I needed to be as close to heaven as possible. Now that I knew for certain that life after death existed, I didn't want to be a ghost; I wanted my heaven: an eternal stage. I couldn't go to prison. No one would want to work with me. No one would hire me again.

The door was still open for the gods. I pushed it closed behind me. All the seats in Draoícht were red, but the colour had eyes up here. I walked to the railing. I was just at the edge of the red seats when the guards arrived. What a shame they had missed the performance. They'd be a bit more awe-struck if they had seen me.

"Lacey Lane?" one of them asked. "We need to talk to you about—" He stopped what he was going to say when he saw how near I was to the railing. I placed my hand on the top bar. The metal was cool under my skin.

"She follows me everywhere," I said. The guards looked at each other.

"Who follows you?" asked a guard with chiselled cheekbones and dark brown hair.

"Natalie," I said. "She follows me everywhere." I swung my leg over the railing. The guards walked faster. I held up my hand. "Stop, or I'll go over. I mean it, I will." I would go over anyway. They'd be fools to think I wouldn't.

"Everything's going to be okay," said a guard with Icelandic blond hair and eyes.

I laughed. "Do you know I wasn't going to be Lady

Macbeth? Natalie Sadowski was meant to play her, but she died in September. Did ye know that?"

"It was tragic," said the blonde guard.

"How did she die?" I asked.

Neither of them wanted to engage with me. You could see it in their faces. "Tell me, or I'll go over," I said.

"She choked on her vomit," said the dark-haired guard.

"That's right. In Red Lane. She was there dead for hours until her flatmate, Lisa, came and found her. She was on her way to work; she wasn't even looking for Natalie. There's the cosmic hand of the universe in full effect," I laughed.

Neither guard said anything.

"I was in Red Lane before Lisa arrived. Hours before she did. Natalie was alive then. She must've sat down for a rest on the walk home. She was sitting on the grass when I saw her, fast asleep and coughing away. Mad for me to follow in her steps, wasn't it?"

"She was still alive?" the blonde-haired guard asked.

"She was an insomniac; I didn't know that. The drink sent her into lullaby land. Poor Natalie. I wonder if she dreamed as she choked. Couldn't've been nice dreams; she looked terrified."

"Are you saying you watched her choke?"

I don't know which guard asked me. I was back there on that night, seeing the figure on the grass. It was the Plague Doctor. It was. Then it wasn't. It was only Natalie. I knew she was choking, but I didn't help her. I kept my phone's torch pointed at her. At least she died with the spotlight on her. "I did," I said. "She took my role."

The guards had snuck up on me. They were standing just a foot away now. I sat up on the gold bar. My hands were wet with sweat. Just a tilt back the way, and I'd be gone. "But I never meant to hurt Evie." I could see her in her elf ears, trembling as she told me about Jess. She couldn't keep it a secret anymore. She said it was killing her. Then she morphed into the Plague Doctor. "I love Evie. She tricked me." I pointed at Natalie, and I lost my balance. My heart leapt too, flying closer to the gods. The guards grabbed me and pulled me towards them.

"She won't leave me alone." I was crying now. I was not a pretty crier. Mam always told me this. "I hate you, Natalie." I went to lunge for her, and the guards pulled me back. They couldn't see her. They didn't know my agony.

Natalie put back on her mask and faded until only a cold spot was left. I could feel it even with all the pulling and thrashing I was doing. Yes, I watched Natalie die. My only regret is I didn't kill her with my own hands.

"Evie," I said. "Is she awake?"

"She is," the blonde guard said. "And she's claiming that you pushed her."

"I didn't mean to," I cried.

I could see the stage. I could see it well—my stage. The guards pulled me away and led me down the stairs. Mam waited at the bottom step.

"Lacey," she said. She was crying. I'd never seen Mam cry.

That night, lying in the cell that stank of bleach, I could still see my stage and hear the applause of my ovation. I was brilliant.

I am brilliant.

The End

ABOUT THE AUTHOR

J.M Clerkin lives in the southeast of Ireland. When she is not reading or writing, you can find her exploring Ireland and beyond.

ACKNOWLEDGEMENTS

Thank you to everyone who read this story and helped make it better. And thank you for reading my book.